THE WEST WIND

Also by Faith Baldwin
in Large Print:

Rehearsal for Love
Something Special
The Office Wife
Make-Believe
The Heart Remembers
District Nurse
Breath of Life
Beauty
The Rest of My Life With You
You Can't Escape
Innocent Bystander
He Married a Doctor

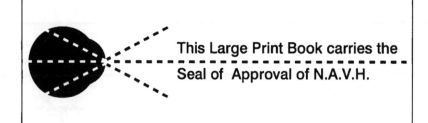

This Large Print Book carries the
Seal of Approval of N.A.V.H.

THE WEST WIND

FAITH BALDWIN

Thorndike Press • Thorndike, Maine

55223

Published in 1998 by arrangement with
Harold Ober Associates, Inc.

Thorndike Large Print® Candlelight Series.

The tree indicium is a trademark of Thorndike Press.

The text of this Large Print edition is unabridged.
Other aspects of the book may vary from the original edition.

Set in 16 pt. Plantin by Al Chase.

Printed in the United States on permanent paper.

Library of Congress Cataloging in Publication Data
Baldwin, Faith, 1893–
    The west wind : a novel / by Faith Baldwin.
      p. cm.
    ISBN 0-7862-1548-8 (lg. print : hc : alk. paper)
    1. Large type books. I. Title.
    [PS3505.U97W47   1998]
    813′.52—dc21   98-25652

For Paul Hervey Fox
Glückliche Reise ——

FOREWORD

In July, 1952, I read in *Time* magazine, an extract from a sermon preached at Princeton Theological Seminary by Dr. Clarence Edward Macartney, of the First Presbyterian Church in Pittsburgh. I copied the extract, and wrote Dr. Macartney, asking him if I could use his interpretation of the West wind in a novel. On July 25 of that year he answered, giving me permission.

Here is the extract:

> Preach all the four winds . . . preach the North wind of God's righteous judgments . . . that the way of the transgressor is hard, and the wages of sin is death. Preach the East wind of God's affliction, that whom He loveth He chasteneth and scourgeth. Preach the South wind of temptation and danger. But, most of all, preach the West wind. You're never really preaching until you're preaching the West wind of God's mercy and pity and forgiveness.

Dr. Macartney died some years ago. Perhaps had he lived to read this novel he would not have liked it . . . but I must make this acknowledgment, with gratitude.

And also to another preacher, one who lived many years ago, an Italian, Savonarola, who perished at the stake and once said, ". . . do not forgive and forget; forgive and *remember*."

CHAPTER 1

On a certain night in early April, Lewis Davies Jones was unfaithful to his wife, Margaret.

In the fourteen years of their marriage there had been no precedent. This event — or, if you prefer, act — had cast no shadow before it, being unpremeditated. It was also, in itself, as unimportant as the quiet fall of a leaf in autumn, which even the tree does not recognize as a signal of altering seasons.

Lewis Davies Jones, called Davy by those who knew him best, was sales manager of a New England company which manufactured plastics. It was a big, prosperous company, and part of his job was to attend conferences, consult with customers and remedy, if possible, any failures of the salesmen.

On this blue-brushed April evening, Davy was on his way home, driving a small foreign car. He had planned to arrive late that night, but he was tired. This morning's customer — the last of the three he'd seen on this trip — had been more difficult than he'd anticipated. He thought: It can't have been entirely Dick's fault. . . . The client, nevertheless, had complained bitterly of the young salesman who had his district.

Davy thought: I'll talk to Dick about this, of course, but not to Bemis. Dick has enough trouble with his wife's extravagance and the second kid en route, to say nothing of the usual mortgage and in-laws. That talk could wait until he had reported to George Bemis, who was his superior.

Looking at the darkening sky, where one pure star hung suspended in the dusk, Davy thought of his wife — most people called her Meg — and of her light, sweet voice over the wire when he had called her earlier to say, "Don't expect me until shortly before noon tomorrow."

She'd been disappointed — as she always was when he had to stay away longer than he planned — but she accepted the factors of fatigue and the considerable distance he still had to cover. She'd wanted to know if anything had happened and he'd answered, no, he'd just run into a snag; he added, hastily that it had been overcome after discussion and the expenditure of more time than he'd allotted. Meg, he knew very well, was a worrier; she worried, he thought, smiling a little, in several directions — backward, forward, even sideways. Once, Mike Miller, their physician and friend, had remarked to him that Meg was innately insecure. Davy knew this, and it saddened him. She had everything his love, protection, and comparative success could give her. He wondered often if, in the majority of childless marriages, the women felt insecure.

After he'd talked with her, he drove on until after twilight. The highway was monotonous, but before it grew dark, he could, by looking briefly away from the hypnotic stretches, see the green-misted boughs and the delicate footprints of spring in the grass. This day, following cold, wet weather, had been warm and gracious, a promising sort of day. Now and then a bird flashed across the road, flying from the safety of one branch or field to another.

Having made no overnight reservation, Davy went on until he saw, near the highway, a motel which looked pleasant enough. He turned off at the indicated exit and into a circular drive, parked his car, and went into the lobby-office. Yes, said the clerk, they had accommodations; no, they hadn't a restaurant, but down the road a mile or so he'd find a good one. Davy registered and was shown his room in the middle of a string of cubicles. It was, like most motel rooms, impersonal. The painted metal furniture was standard, but the curtains were fresh and gay. There was the advertised wall-to-wall carpeting — with here and there a cigarette burn — and a television set, a table model with the long ears which always reminded him of something out of science fiction. For the rest: twin beds, a night table, a desk-*cum*-bureau, three chairs — one comfortable — and adequate lighting.

He thought of all the faceless people who inhabit motel rooms, coming and going as briefly and easily as birds light on the branch and then depart; people who leave nothing behind them except the cigarette burns, a sock perhaps, handkerchiefs, small gear but nothing of themselves, no clue to their personalities. People could have been born or died, could have been murdered or seduced in this room, he reflected; they could have shut the door and closed themselves in with sorrow or happiness, yet have left no impression. Houses were different — except the very new ones; eventually they adapted to their owners. In his own house, which was middle-aged, he had always a sense of something or someone other than Meg and himself having lived there quietly and harmoniously.

He went into the bathroom which had — also advertised — both tub and shower. Looking about, he deplored the magenta tiling.

A methodical man, he unpacked, absently noting that heat had been provided, and glad of it, as April nights turn chilly. There was also, though not yet necessary, air conditioning. Presently he sat down at the desk and added to the brief report he'd written during his conversation — if it could be called that — with the last customer. Then he undressed and showered. He'd have to shave now and again tomorrow morning, he thought, sighing as he looked at his face under the fluorescent light above the mirror, passing his hand over his chin.

He was a dark man, whose Welsh ancestry was evident; his grandfather had been born in Glamorganshire. Davy in no way resembled his blonde, fair-skinned mother, or his brothers. He looked more like his grandfather than he did like his father; and he remembered his grandfather well.

When Davy was small and became entangled in some special mischief, his grandfather would say, tolerantly, "He's a little fey, our Davy."

Now, shaved and dressed, he got into his car and went in search of the restaurant, which proved to be a commonplace, clean structure with a dining room, a bar, and recorded music.

The dining room was crowded and, before

the hostess could reach him, he made his way to the bar, where he sat talking to the bartender over a Scotch and water. When, moderately hungry, he went back to the dining room, there was still only one vacant chair, at a table occupied by a woman.

The hostess came up, saying, "I'll have a table in just a moment, sir."

"Thanks," said Davy and smiled at her. He was not a particularly good-looking man, being a little too tall and a little too thin and having features that had been rather carelessly assembled. His attraction lay in the enormous vitality of extremely dark eyes and a slow smile. He added, "I'll wait in the bar."

He gave the hostess his name and she promised to call him.

He returned to the bar, had his second light drink, and once more engaged the bartender in conversation. They spoke of the bad winter, now mercifully past — "but I remember a hell of a blizzard one April," said the bartender gloomily — and of the chances for a good spring. "We don't have them fine, old-fashioned springs no more," commented the bartender, and then they talked of business, the bartender inevitably describing his as lousy.

When the hostess came to say, "Mr.

14

Jones," Davy paid his tab and followed her. At the door he encountered the woman who had been alone at what would now be, briefly, his table. They glanced at each other and Davy said, "I hope I didn't hurry you." She said "No. I was just finishing."

She was, he saw, a small woman; of his age perhaps, possibly older. Her hair was an improbable red and her smile impersonal.

Davy ordered and ate his dinner, which was mediocre, took his time over the coffee, which was surprisingly good, and then returned to the motel.

There was a pile of New York newspapers on the office desk. He bought one, glancing at the headlines which were, as usual, depressing. In one way or another, whether stated soberly or sensationally, the world appeared to be going to hell in a hand basket. Standing by the desk, he turned to the financial pages. His investments were not spectacular, but they were sound. The sensitive tides of Wall Street, rising and falling, affected him personally very little. And when an occasional gambling instinct seized him, his broker, an old friend, curbed him with a definite, "Now if I were you, Davy . . ."

He returned to his room, where he'd left, on the bedside table, a couple of paperback mysteries. He picked one up and riffled the pages without interest. He did not feel like reading, it was too early to sleep, and he was bored. What he needed was a walk. He wished that Corky, his springer spaniel, were with him.

He took off his jacket, hung it up, turned on the bedside light, moved the ash tray, lay down and opened the other book. After a while he tossed it on the bed and rose.

He put on his jacket again and went out. The motel was on a main road leading into the nearest town. Walking on it would be tedious and unhealthy. But there were grounds around the motel, and at the back, the ubiquitous, small swimming pool.

Davy walked to the pool and around it. The grounds blazed with light, and the cement-lined excavation was exposed in all its naked desolation of emptiness. Few in-animate objects are more depressing, he thought. He whistled absent-mindedly, on key, and felt for a cigarette.

As he found the pack and lit one, he heard footsteps and turned to see the woman who had been in the restaurant.

"Hi," he said.

She smiled. "May I borrow your matches?" she asked. "I never seem to have any and I always forget to fill my lighter."

Davy offered her his pack, but she shook

her head. "I smoke my own brand," she said, and produced it as he offered the match flame. In its brief, close illumination he saw that her face was more lined than he'd noticed when they passed each other in the dining-room doorway . . . not, he thought, with age but, rather, with tensions.

She asked, "It was you in the restaurant?" and when he nodded, added, "Dinner wasn't much, was it? I couldn't sleep and I've a long way to travel tomorrow. So I came out for some air." She lifted her head and took a long breath. "I can smell the spring and I don't like it," she said flatly.

Possibly she expected an answer or an argument. He didn't know, so contented himself with remarking gravely that all seasons were all things to all men.

That didn't make sense, he reflected, smiling to himself, but it sounded philosophical.

"Let's sit down," the woman suggested abruptly.

There were some benches nearby from which presumably, in season, one watched transient swimmers on hot summer days or evenings.

They sat down on the nearest one, smoked and talked — desultory small talk — what was or was not happening in the world, weather, motels, the fortunes of the road.

And after a while she rose, stretched, and bent her head back. "I can't get rid of the kink in my neck," she complained.

"Driving does it," said Davy.

"Whether I'm driving or not," she answered, as she began to walk away. Davy followed and before they reached the motel she said, "Come in for a nightcap."

He hesitated for a second. Well, why not? But before he could speak, she said, "Ships that pass in the night." As banal as her hair.

He thought: Not exactly. Not any more. Rather Volkswagens, Buicks, Jaguars, Fords — which pass in the morning.

He said, "Fine," and went with her to her room, the last one opening from the long porch. They met no one and if anyone saw them, it was without curiosity.

Her room could have been his own; the only differences were the cosmetic case open on the bureau-desk, a pair of dainty bedroom slippers on the floor, and across one bed, a bedjacket, a nightgown, and a frilly robe. On the night table there were several paperback books.

She went into the clothes closet and emerged with a bottle. There was on her bureau, as on his, a pitcher and two glasses on a heavy, round, glass tray. She said,

18

"There's an ice machine right outside. I don't use it."

Davy picked up the pitcher and went out to the machine. Returning, he knocked, and she said, "Come in." When he had, she walked past him and closed the door. She said, "I hope you aren't allergic to bourbon."

"Not to anything alcoholic," he answered, "provided it's in moderation."

"Suppose you fix your own," she said and poured herself a drink, the size of which startled him. She took the pitcher into the bathroom, filled it, and splashed a little water in her glass. "You can fish your ice out," she said indifferently.

She sat down in the armchair and Davy pulled up the chair from the desk and said, "To tomorrow's journey."

"To yours," she said, and drank.

"Why not to your own?" he asked, smiling.

"It's always the same," she said vaguely. "You leave one place and go to another."

There was a short silence and then Davy said, "I haven't asked your name."

"It's Vivian."

"Is that all?"

"No, but it's as much as is necessary — it's a thousand, a million, to one we'll never see each other again. If we do, you can just yell, 'Hi, Vivian.' "

" 'Answer to "Hi," or to any loud cry . . .' " he said, and when she looked at him blankly, added hastily, "Just an old quotation I picked up in a motel room."

"You haven't told me your name," she reminded him.

"Lewis."

"First or last?"

Now it was beginning to be a game. "You made the rules," he reminded her. "Does it matter?"

"Of course not."

Davy was a little amused and then thoughtful. Possibly he read too many mysteries when he was out on the road. Suppose she was being pursued by the law, an outraged husband, or a cast-off lover . . . ?

He laughed.

"So what's funny?" she inquired.

"Nothing, really. I was just thinking, I read too much blood and thunder or watch too much suspense on TV."

She had perception or perhaps merely common sense. "So do I," she said, "and I thought that, too."

"What?"

"What you were thinking. But you don't look as if you were playing cops and robbers. And I'm not escaping from anything" — she

20

paused — "at least not from anything that could put me behind bars or leave me with a bullet. . . . How about another drink?"

He shook his head. "Thanks, no. I had a couple before dinner at the restaurant bar."

"So did I," she said, "and a three-year-old could have managed them."

He wondered if she would presently ask him the usual questions: Are you married? What do you do? Where do you live? Have you children? Anything short of "What's your full name?" But she did not. She rose and made herself another drink, remarking only, "You're from New England."

"Is it so obvious?"

"Oh, yes, in your accent" — she set down her generous drink and smiled at him; she seemed relaxed now, and looked five years younger — "and maybe in your mouth, but not your eyes."

"Can you explain that?" he asked.

"Not exactly. Still, I'm used to — well — sizing up people in my job."

"Should I ask what your job is? I'm sure it's interesting."

"No; and it isn't, really."

"All right." He looked at her hands, noticing for the first time that she wore no rings except a heavy engraved stone of some sort on the little finger of her right hand. Her hands did not look as if they worked; they were well kept, well shaped, although he did not like the color of her nail polish, which matched her lipstick. But then he didn't like nail polish period.

He wondered about her job. There are so many jobs in which it is necessary to evaluate people.

"You haven't explained how my ancestry shows, beyond the accent," he reminded.

She said, "Well, your mouth is firm, and cautious" — she regarded him a moment; her eyes were neither gray nor blue — "and kind, I think. But your eyes aren't cautious. They give you away. For instance, you don't approve of how much I drink."

"I don't approve or disapprove."

"I'm not an alcoholic yet," she remarked thoughtfully. "I don't think I shall be, really, if — before I reach that stage, the time comes when I won't need crutches or escape hatches."

"I hope it does," he said sincerely. "You're a young woman."

"Forty's young?"

"Yes."

"That's outside," she said dreamily. "Inside, you can be sixty-five or eighteen, God help you."

He nodded and rose, setting down his

glass. He said, "I've enjoyed this. Now I'd better turn in. Thanks for the drink, and good luck on the road, Vivian."

She rose also, and with her glass again in her hand, moved close to him. "Please don't go," she said. Involuntarily he stepped back, and she added, "Please stay. There are — other forms of escape, and as I said, your mouth is kind."

So it happened — if anything really happens — like that, impersonally and, like the falling leaf, without importance.

CHAPTER 2

Davy walked back to his room along the porch corridor. The night was moonless but thickly starred. He encountered no one, and his footfall was habitually light. Here and there, on either side of the office, lights still burned in the rooms. He could hear the blurred sound of cars on the highway and, closer, on the road which snaked past the motel. Two cars turned in as he unlocked his door; tired people who had driven too far, seeking comfortable beds and a few hours' sleep.

He opened his door and looked with incredulity at this room which, not long since, he had left to walk beside an empty pool. He had paid for this room when he registered. Presently he would leave it and, God grant, he would never see it again.

Everything was as he had left it: the urban newspaper on the desk, the bedside lamp still burning, the mystery book on the bed which bore the faint imprint of his long body.

Here, as in all the other rooms, including the one at the far end of the corridor, the evidences of personality were trivial. Entering this room — or the other — you'd be aware only of the sex of the transient occupant. Duplicate rooms, one used casually by a man, the other by a woman. In the bathroom, he smelled his shaving lotion and remembered, with a knot of nausea in his throat, that only as he had left that other room had he become sharply aware of scent: soap, powder, perfume, a whisper of fragrance, laced with the odor of whisky.

Although he was usually considerate, he showered, not caring whether sleeping neighbors would be awakened by the rush of water. The thick lather of the soap washed away once, twice; but still he was not clean.

No excuses, no blame transferred, nothing but an immense fatigue in his blood and bones and, in the appalled repudiation of his mind, the unbelief.

He went to bed, snapped off the light and flung his arms over his head. The porch lights shone in and made relentless, abstract patterns on the walls. He thought heavily: I can't sleep. Yet he did so, almost at once, hardly stirring and not dreaming; or, if he dreamed, he did not, on waking, remember.

People generally leave motels early; they want to be on their way. It was not much past daylight when Davy turned in his key.

The clerk asked cheerfully, "Did you have a comfortable night?" and Davy nodded. "We pride ourselves on our beds," said the clerk. He added, glancing at the register, "You're making an early start, Mr. Jones. How about one for the road? There's a coffee machine right over there."

David said, "Thanks, I think I'll go on." He was desperate to get away; he wanted out. Any moment Vivian might come walking into the lobby on her high heels.

He returned to his car, into which he'd already put his luggage, and took off. He drove carefully and automatically, and did not feel the evanescent freshness of the April morning, sweet and cool, the sky clotted with white altering clouds.

After a while he stopped at a highway restaurant, went to a counter and drank two cups of black coffee. The waitress regarded him with interest. She hadn't worked here, or anywhere else, long enough to be indifferent to the customers streaming in, always in a hurry, looking at the dog-eared menus, restlessly awaiting service, ringing tips on the counter, streaming out again. Hers was a new, small world of voices, color, noise.

This tall man was silent except for, "Good morning. Just coffee, please," and a little later, "I'll have another cup, if I may." She was too new to know quite how to make conversation which, at this time of morning, would have been possible, since there were not many customers.

He said, "Good-by," and left change on the counter, more than the coffee had cost, paid his check at the cash register — that girl looked at the check and not at him; she'd worked here a long time — and went out to have gas put in his tank. To the routine query, "Check your oil and water, sir?" he nodded, thinking of the miles ahead and knowing that his thoughts must companion him.

When, before noon, he drove into the town in which he lived and through it, to a secondary road, and eventually turned into his own driveway, he felt as if he had driven across the continent without stopping.

Corky came tearing out of the open door. He did not bark; he knew the sound of the engine. He fell upon his master with small expressions of rapture and Davy touched the silky head. He said, "Hi, boy."

Davy took his small bag and attaché case from the trunk and went into the house, with Corky leaping about him. Someone was in the kitchen. He thought, mechanically: It isn't Mrs. Lowry's day.

He cleared his throat and called "Meg,"

adding the superfluous phrase, heard so often in every house in the world, "I'm home."

She came swiftly from the kitchen into the hall; she was always swift in movement and gesture.

"Darling," she said, "I didn't hear the car . . . that is, I did, but I thought it was the milkman. He's late." She kissed him. "I'm glad you're home."

He put his bag at the foot of the stairs. "I had an early start," he told her.

"How about coffee? Are you going on to the plant? Will you have lunch there?" she asked.

"Yes." He walked into the living room and looked at it as if he had never seen it before. He put his attaché case on the desk. "I want to see Bemis," he told his wife, "before he leaves for his plane this afternoon."

Bemis, the general manager, lived not far up the road in a house older than this one.

"I was going to make you a steak sandwich," said Meg, disappointed. "I got those special tid-bits you like."

"Tomorrow," he said. He usually came home for lunch unless Meg was out.

"Coffee?" she asked again. "I'll put it right on."

"Fine. I'll be down in a minute." He

touched her bright brown hair, went to the hall, picked up his bag, and went upstairs.

When he had reached the big bedroom they shared, he looked about, much as he had in the living room. A strange thought crossed his mind: They would never really share it again.

Nonsense. Nothing's changed. I'm just dog-tired.

The ceiling in this room, as all in the house, was high. There were four windows. Outside of one, the tall lilac had dark buds and on the maples the beginning leaves were red.

There were flowers in the room. Meg loved and grew them. When her garden slept, she bought them. "One of my minor extravagances," she'd say. Here, as downstairs, there were jonquils and hyacinths, which were too heavily scented.

Meg had a nice feeling for furniture; throughout the house were things she had bought over a long period of time, in off-highway shops, at auctions, on their trips together. In the bedroom, mostly maple, old and polished, and a good deal of milk glass.

Her bedside table held the books she was reading. They were no clue to her character. She read for, and usually with, pleasure, although in recent years often with disgust,

29

tossing aside the current library book. Her taste was catholic, and of no special significance: romance; fictionalized biography; a little easy, do-it-yourself, all's-well-with-the-world philosophy; and books which dealt with religion in a simple way — not difficult to grasp, not those which took God apart and then tried to put Him together again . . . the Humpty Dumpty God of the era.

Davy looked at the glazed chintz curtains and the bedspreads, which were quilts, in the wedding-ring pattern. They had belonged to Meg's grandmother. "You take them," her sister Amy had said. She was ten years older than Meg and had brought her up. Meg went to her with everything.

Now Davy ceased to observe and to think. He merely felt. He was a stranger in a strange room.

An hour, two hours — how long? a century perhaps, or ten minutes, time being psychological — spent in another strange room and he had returned to his own house, one which he had chosen, bought and paid for, and now it no longer seemed to know or acknowledge him.

Meg called up the stairs. "Aren't you ever coming down, dear?"

There was no longer an excuse to stay up here. He had shaved before leaving the mo-

30

tel. So he went down and sat opposite his wife at the kitchen table, in the sunny utilitarian room, and they talked as they always did when he returned from a trip he'd taken alone.

Now she said, "I wish I'd gone with you. They postponed the committee meeting."

"Why?" he asked, as the question was expected of him, thinking: Meg, Meg, if only you had been with me. For she often went when the trip was not too tedious, and while he was busy, she would prowl around whatever town they were in, window-shop and find, here and there, a bargain.

Meg's coffee was very good. She asked, "Where'd you stay last night? I thought maybe you'd call. The Collinses were over for a while. Their TV's out of order and there was a program they wanted to see."

He told her where he had stayed or, rather, near what town. He could not remember the name of the motel, although the bill stamped "paid" was in his attaché case for the expense account. With fleeting grim humor he wondered if the place were called "Bide-a-Wee," or "Travelers' Rest," or starkly, "Highway Motel."

"Was it nice?" Meg asked.

"Like any good motel," he answered and yawned suddenly.

31

"You're tired, Davy."

"A little," he admitted.

"Where did you eat last night? Was there a restaurant connected with the motel?"

"No . . . but a decent enough place down the road," he said. These were questions he'd heard and answered for a long time; ordinary questions, prompted, he knew, by genuine interest, not merely routine. Now they were like small darts, penetrating his mind.

"Try to come home early," Meg urged, "and take a nap before dinner. Helen and Bob are coming. Remember?"

He'd forgotten. These were their closest friends, the Watsons. The women, engaged in civic projects together, were constantly in and out of each other's houses; they shared enthusiasms; the men golfed and played poker; all four played contract and almost every summer they rented a vacation cottage together on a lake in Vermont.

The Watsons had children, three uninhibited youngsters.

Davy pushed back his chair and said, "I'd better change my shirt."

"It looks clean," Meg said, smiling judiciously. She was nearly a beautiful woman, but not quite.

"Oh, driving . . ." he explained vaguely.

He'd put on a fresh shirt that morning. Now he went up, took it off, and found another in his drawer.

He sat down on his bed and took a cigarette from a Staffordshire mug on his night table. The matching mug was on Meg's. He remembered where she'd bought them, one bright blue autumn day, in a place a hundred and fifty miles distant, and how when he'd returned to the motel from a conference, she was admiring them on the commonplace bureau. "Such a bargain!" she cried when he came in. "I'd have paid twice as much in most places."

He looked down at the books beside him: a volume of Dylan Thomas — Meg didn't like poetry — and, in contrast, one of Robert Frost, and a book on the current political situation. He thought idly that books on political or international situations were obsolete almost as soon as published.

Then he went downstairs, kissed his wife, and went out to the car. She followed him, wearing a bulky sweater over her pink cotton frock. "It's cold," she said, "but things are coming out. After you're rested, perhaps we can walk around before dinner?"

They had about an acre, much of it wooded.

Davy drove into town and across to the

plant. It was a big, contemporary building, with light, air, space, and color; the grounds were landscaped and by the river there was a picnic place to which many of the employees brought their lunches on fine days. The cafeteria inside was as good, or better, than most and the executives' dining room — used only on special occasions — had been photographed half a dozen times for the magazines. This was considered a model plant. There was rarely difficulty with the unions. The employees worked in an atmosphere which was, in the main, harmonious, and they had many advantages. The pension plan, bonuses, and pay, were good; there were adequate vacations and hospitalization. Davy had worked here for ten years. He had had, in the last two, several offers from other firms, but he was not interested. The Board had made him sales manager three years ago and when Bemis retired, Davy would be in line for the general managership, a position which carried with it a vice-presidency, as well as more money.

Now he drove into the parking lot and spoke to the man there. "How's the kid?" he asked.

The man said, "Better, thanks," and watched him walk away, thinking: He's a good Joe.

34

In the open, first-floor section, everything was as usual. People spoke to Davy from their desks. "Hi, Mr. J., how did it go?"

"Fine, Henry," said Davy. "Nice day, isn't it?"

He was not alone in the self-service elevator and a couple of men and one woman said, "Hi, Davy." In the upper echelons the use of given names was the custom. He entered his own office and Mrs. Easton, his excellent secretary, not young but very well turned out, greeted him and added, "Mr. Bemis has been on the phone."

"Tell him I'll be right in," he said. He glanced at the IN basket and shuddered. No matter how brief a time you were away from it, the IN basket, opening its greedy maw, sat there and waited.

He squared his shoulders, which were somewhat broader and heavier than one would expect of a man of his build, and went into Bemis' office to report on the past few days. He had everything with him in the brief case: figures, problems, and suggested solutions.

He'd never been so glad to see Bemis, sixty, getting heavy, going bald, wearing rimless glasses on a short, abrupt nose.

After the usual give and take between men who work together, know and respect each other, Davy opened his case and put his papers on the big, uncluttered desk. Close to a semi-starved IN basket, a gold pen and pencil set stood chastely, the inscription on its onyx base clear and plain: "George Bemis — twenty-five years of service." On the opposite corner of the desk were pictures of Bemis' wife, Ethel, and their children. Davy had sat on the visitor's side of this desk innumerable times. Now and then, in recent years, it had given him quick anticipatory pleasure to think that someday he would sit behind it. He didn't experience it today. He was simply glad to see George and to be briefly free of personal preoccupations.

He thought: I won't speak to him about Dick . . . the kid rates another chance. I'll talk to him myself.

"Looks as if you'd had a rough time," Bemis said, reading the report. "But Gilligan's a tough man. Very."

"It was all right," said Davy, and began to talk.

Later he and Bemis went to the cafeteria. There were two places left at the executives' table, and the general conversation was as it usually is with such a group during the lunch hour in the cafeteria of a plant: business outlooks, golf, the world situation, someone's struggles with a house full of measles

— "Can you really have it twice?" asked the father of the stricken brood — inquiries after someone else's wife, hospitalized for observation . . . commonplace talk, repeated all over the country with variations of the themes.

Driving home, after coping with some of the IN-basket demands, and having a quiet talk with young Dick Norton, in from a trip yesterday, Davy thought: I can't live with myself if I don't tell Meg, but if I do tell her, will she be able to live with me?

He knew that — does one say "technically"? — Vivian and the room at the end of the motel corridor were unimportant. "Like a handshake," a man had once said to him years ago — confidingly and a little drunk — or a cup of coffee, or a sudden breeze, rising, then dying down. But he knew Meg would not consider it unimportant. She was a good wife, loving and kind. They'd come to understand each other as well as most married people do. Where their interests differed, each conceded the other's right to such difference, though it had taken a little time on Meg's part. Davy understood her profound grief, colored with resentment — and rarely mentioned now — at not having children. They'd both gone the rounds of the specialists. Just one of those things, was the diagnosis, though not so expressed. He, too, felt the lack and even the need of children, if not in quite the same way. At one time they'd talked of adopting a child or two, but Meg had finally said, "No, an adopted child wouldn't be mine."

He'd reminded her of several couples they knew with adopted children, and how close they were; no children could have been more their own.

"I'd love any child," Meg had said, and so she would; she loved her sister's children and those of her friends, and she worked her head off for children she'd never seen — the forlorn, the neglected, the forgotten. "But, not in the same way."

She meant not in the way she would have loved a child she bore, through whose coming she experienced the mystic awareness of flesh, blood, and bones.

No, he could not tell her about the motel episode. How could he? He could not destroy his image in her mind because he had destroyed it in his own. Lewis Davies Jones, thirty-eight years old; a happy, faithful husband, often exposed to what is known as temptation, as any man is, and during the exposure, amused and a little — what is the exact word? — vain or excited about it, but not interested. Normal reaction is not always purposeful interest. In five words, he was not having any.

This image of himself no longer existed; in the mirror of his mind it was distorted and, to him, unrecognizable.

CHAPTER 3

It was more than absurd, it was neurotic to turn sick at the smell of bourbon, which was the Watsons' drink. To Davy, the familiar pattern of the evening was dreadful because it was so familiar: the friendly card game, the relaxed talk, the compatible silences, the family-type jokes. When people know one another well, there are always the jokes which would mean nothing to anyone else.

Then, too, there was the mutual Vermont vacation to discuss. Davy thought, seeing clearly the lake and the cottage: Perhaps when that time comes . . . ?

He saw Bob Watson look at him a time or two and knew he was playing a bad game, which as a rule he didn't. He and Bob always played against their wives and kept a running score which was never settled, "any more than the national debt," as Bob had once remarked.

The room looked the same . . . the pleasant room; the card table was the same . . . a solid table. The Watsons were the same . . . a good, devoted couple. Bob was a successful, small-town lawyer, attractive and understanding; his wife, Helen, a pretty, round woman, charming and amiable.

Once, when he was dummy, Davy rose and moved a vase of hyacinths farther away and when Meg asked, frowning a little over her cards, "What was that for?" he said, "They're awfully heavy, or is it me?"

"You," said Bob cheerfully.

When the final rubber was over, Bob asked, "You feel all right, Davy?"

"Sure." He added, "Why?" because one always asks why.

"You look a little off color and, boy, what a lousy game! Not that it alarms me; we're still light years ahead of the girls."

"Don't judge me by my game," said Davy.

In contrast to Bob's careful, shrewd game, Davy's usually annoyed his opponents; it was not always orthodox, though often intuitively brilliant and sparked with what is called luck.

"He's tired," Meg said, and her blue-gray eyes clouded with anxiety. She thought: Has something happened that he hasn't told me? Business? The stock market? It couldn't be business unless he was keeping something from her. She'd made it a project to understand a good deal about the plant. The stock market? She knew less than nothing about that. His health? Perhaps he'd had a check-

41

up and hadn't told her and had sworn Mike Miller to secrecy. Perhaps the occasional discomfort of which he complained was more serious than indigestion. His heart? Meg had the vivid imagination of most worriers, and a mind which magnified trifles.

Now she and Helen went to the kitchen and brought in crackers and cheese for the second and final drink of the evening. Corky, who had been asleep somewhere, came galloping in for his snack, and after a while the Watsons left. Next week's game would be at their house.

When the doors had been locked and the downstairs lights were out, Meg and Davy went upstairs, Corky pattering after them. His cushion was in the corner of the hall, so that, even in his sleep, he could keep an eye upon the house and his people.

Meg waited until Davy had undressed and yawned his way to bed before she asked, "Is there anything on your mind, dear?"

"Just sleep. What else would there be?"

"Conscience" is usually just a word to most people. One frequently hears it from the pulpit. You believe it exists, of course, but you manage not to experience it too often. Experienced, it can be an ulcer, eating its way through you with its own peculiar acid.

"I don't know, but Bob said —"

He interrupted irritably, "For God's sake, Meg, can't any of you understand that I'm just tired. You said so yourself."

He was given to sudden, quick tempers, soon over and always regretted, but never to petulance or irritability. She thought: Something *is* the matter. Tomorrow, at the Free Clinic, to which she gave a certain amount of time, she might run into Mike Miller and then she could ask him casually, "Has Davy been in to see you lately?"

But if Davy had asked him not to tell her . . . ?

She was both hurt and troubled and after a moment she said, "Good night, dear," in what he often called her little girl voice, a voice which meant he had hurt her.

"Good night, Meg." He wanted to say, "I'm sorry I was sharp with you," but couldn't.

Neither slept for some time, but did not again speak to each other.

Before Meg slept, she said her silent prayers. Her personal religion was comforting and inexacting and she trusted it. She approached a wise, vague, but benevolent Maker as a child its parent, rather in the way she'd always gone to Amy.

Amy had been a thoughtful, practical ten-year-old when Meg was born and had accepted her as a flesh-and-blood doll to be dressed, undressed, fed, scolded, loved, spoiled — and also, directed. No other children had been born in the decade which separated them, and their mother had died when Meg was two. Amy explained the age difference to her sister when Meg was able to understand: "Mother was always delicate, so she and Dad didn't plan any children after me, though they were sorry to bring up an only."

That was a tactical error, because Meg thereafter thought of herself as a mistake; she was comforted, however, by the thought that, at least, Amy had wanted her.

Two years after their mother died, their father — whom Amy resembled, being kind, unimaginative, and handsome — remarried. His second wife, whom his children liked, soon was so busy bringing up her own children that she was content to have Amy assume full responsibility for Meg.

Therefore, when Meg prayed, she prayed to a distant, masculine, omnipotent Amy. Now she asked, in her mind: Please don't let Davy be ill; please don't let anything happen to him; please make things right.

She didn't know what was wrong, or if,

indeed, anything was . . . but should it be, she wanted it made right.

Morning had the appearance of answered prayer: the sun shone, blackbirds whistled, and a robin predicted firmly that it was not going to rain.

Meg woke first and looked across at her husband. Sleeping, he seemed innocent and defenseless, his face smooth except for the two perpendicular lines between his eyebrows, rather like a proofreader's mark, which were always there. He really was just tired, she assured herself and went in to shower.

Davy woke, hearing the sound of it and, for a second, wondered where he'd recently heard water falling like a small Niagara of doom. . . . Then he remembered.

When Meg came back into the room, he asked, "Isn't it pretty early?" and smiled at her, the characteristic smile which could still turn her heart over. It was no effort to smile at Meg this morning; fresh from the shower, lately out of dreams, you'd have to smile at her from your heart no matter what went on in your mind.

"Mrs. Lowry," Meg said briefly. She crossed the room to kiss him and then whisked into some clothes and was off downstairs. When breakfast was over, she'd get out the station wagon to fetch the formidable, capable Mrs. Lowry, who would, on arrival, go through the house, as was her twice weekly custom, like a fresh spring breeze.

Davy lay still. He heard Meg speak to Corky and though the door was closed, he knew Corky was up on his parti-colored feathered feet and following Meg downstairs.

Possibly Davy had arrived at a conclusion as he slept, for he thought now: I'll put it out of my mind as if it had never happened.

After a while he went downstairs, had breakfast, told Meg a story he'd heard while he was away, asked what was at the movies and were they doing anything that evening?

When they went out to the cars, the little one fairly new, the big one somewhat battered, he held her hand and talked about crabgrass. Something would have to be done about it this year. They hadn't had their tour of the estate yesterday, he reminded her laughing . . . perhaps after he came home this afternoon. . . . The wind was high this morning, and a brown leaf from a tenacious oak tree hopped ahead of them like a minuscule rabbit.

At the Clinic that afternoon, Meg saw Dr.

Miller, who gave of his time as did the other medical men in town, in a rotating service. Her particular volunteer duty was making out forms and talking to anxious mothers, who often had to be reassured or consoled.

She managed to slide away from the desk during a breathing spell, and run Miller into a corner as he was about to leave.

"Hi," said Mike, who had red hair and more vitality than most men as overworked as he was. "Haven't seen you in months. When are you and Davy coming over for an evening?"

"When are you ever at home for a whole evening?"

He had an impersonal tenderness for pretty women, for all women in fact. He said, "Well, half a loaf — come in for a slice anyway. Ginger will call you. How's your guy?"

"Bushed," Meg answered; "at least he was when he came in last night. He hasn't been in to see you lately, has he?" she asked with elaborate carelessness.

Ah! thought Dr. Miller, and answered, "No — and he's about due for his annual going-over — past due, if I'm not mistaken. I'll have Miss Smithers call him and make an appointment, and no nonsense about it. Why? You worried or something?"

"A little," she admitted. "He still has that pain now and then."

"Only because of what my grandmother called a nervous stomach," Mike said, "and that's as good a term as any. Well, we'll soon see." He looked at his watch, exclaimed "Sufferin' Moses!" and departed, his black bag swinging from his big hand.

So things were as they'd been for years, and Mr. and Mrs. Lewis Davies Jones, talked, ate, and slept together. They went out; they had people in; they took walks and sometimes postponed dinner to drive out in the small car in the periwinkle April dusk and look at houses, old and new, the beginning gardens, the full brooks, and little rivers.

Davy went on another short overnight trip and Meg went with him. There was to her, always, excitement in being away with him in a strange place, seeing a movie in a strange town, or going to a strange, not too noisy, bar for a drink.

But when she asked, "How about a nightcap?" that particular evening, he remembered another evening, another voice, and another world. He felt physically ill and thought: It's no use; you can't erase things as if they had been written on a blackboard.

He couldn't say, "I think I'll skip it — I've a stitch in my side." She'd worry all the rest of the evening and all the way home. He couldn't say, "We had a drink at dinner." They'd had just one and this was hours later, after the movie. He didn't want to suggest, "Let's go back to the hotel and have one sent up," for a bar would be better than a hotel room. So he said, "O.K."

It all began again, as simply as that. Conscience, having been sedated, by a form of rationalization perhaps, stirred and the ache was there, the corroding. He asked himself miserably: How do people forget, really forget?

There was no one of whom he could ask advice. He was a man who had many acquaintances and a few close friends, but who usually kept his own counsel. He was generally outgoing, but he could be silent as well as gay. "He's moody," Amy had remarked when she first met him.

Davy's brothers were older than he and they had never been close. One lived in Puerto Rico; the other in Idaho. Their parents had died, after Davy's marriage, within a few years of each other. Besides, he knew how his brothers would counsel him; big, hearty, successful men, they'd say, "Forget it; it didn't mean a thing."

One afternoon on the way home Davy went into town first to do an errand for Meg and passed the church they attended. He thought of it as her church. He went to services with her, listened to her sing in the choir, and considered many things which he couldn't formulate, for which there were no words. In his feeling for religion there was a flash of mysticism, perhaps inherited. He was not content with prayers and hymns and sermons. He'd never been able to go along with Meg and the minister of the beautiful old church.

Orthodox belief, he thought, in whatever creed, is becoming to and in a woman, provided she isn't a fanatic. But when he thought of religion in relation to himself, it was of something as powerful and as formless as the wind.

He'd been sleeping badly. Several times at the plant he'd lost his temper . . . the last time had been with Dick Norton, and that episode blew up into such proportions that he had to take it to Bemis. It had been straightened out, Norton had been briefed, admonished, and given warning this would be his last opportunity. On one occasion Davy, hunting for something he couldn't find, reduced his usually imperturbable secretary to tears, and somewhat later caused

Bemis to ask, with concern, "When's your vacation coming up, Davy?" He had not mentioned any of this to Meg, although usually he told her anything he thought might interest her concerning the business and also discussed any problem which affected him. He began to walk as delicately as Agag and that takes it out of you, the constant reminding of yourself that you must be careful, you must pull in the reins. He couldn't go on like that, forever.

Now, on impulse, he turned into the church driveway and parked by the study. The minister, Herbert Carstairs, just coming out of the office door, exclaimed, with astonishment he didn't attempt to conceal, "Hello, Davy . . . anything wrong?"

"No . . . that is — yes." Now that he was here, he wanted nothing so much as to escape. He tried to think of an excuse. There was none, so he said, "I thought I'd drop in for a minute if you weren't busy."

"I'm through for the day," Dr. Carstairs said. His secretary had left, the telephone had not rung for ten minutes. He was a passionate gardener and had welcomed a chance to go home, grub and dig, pull weeds and thank Heaven, literally kneeling, that his lines had fallen in so pleasant a place.

Relieved, Davy said, "You go along. I'll

51

come another time."

Dr. Carstairs recognized trouble when he saw it, and his heart was heavy. Not these two, he thought; dear God, not these. Yet what else could be wrong? He knew Davy as a successful man; there were no children to present problems, and as far as he knew Davy and Meg, young and healthy, faced no crisis of illness.

Dr. Carstairs had dealt for many years with unhappy wives and husbands; with difficult, wayward, or emotionally disturbed young people; with every kind of sorrow. So now he said, "Nonsense. Come in, I've lots of time."

Davy's instinct was to run, but there was only one way to move, which was forward, and presently they were in the study and the minister was offering him a cigarette. The study smelled of leather, roses and, faintly, of smoke.

Dr. Carstairs drew his heavy gray eyebrows together and waited. He always let people take their time.

Davy said, "I don't know how to tell you."

"Try . . . from the beginning."

So he tried, and after a while his story was told, in all its stark brevity. He ended, "I have no excuse. Not even of need; not even that."

Now Dr. Carstairs asked, after a moment, "How long have you and Meg been married?"

"Fourteen years."

"From my knowledge of you over the last ten or so, I don't have to ask you if it's been a happy marriage."

"It is one," said Davy.

He thought: And so it is; we differ sometimes, but who does not? I annoy her — well, not exactly . . . I worry her. Perhaps she annoys me. Possibly people aren't meant to live together day in, day out. . . . That's silly. Of course they are if they love each other. That was one statement he could make with full assurance. So he made it now, before Carstairs spoke again. He said, "We love each other."

"In which case," Carstairs said, "you share. Love always shares. What are you trying to ask me, Davy — whether or not you should tell her?"

"Yes." He hesitated and then said it again. "Yes," adding, "I can't live with myself. For a while I thought I could, and I tried. But," he ended painfully, "it wasn't any good, the trying."

And Herbert Carstairs, leaning back, thought of the human spirit in every man, of the measuring merciless self-judgment which torments so many, and silently asked for direction.

He said, "Let's look at it as impartially as possible. Sometimes it's kinder to be silent — kinder to the other fellow if not to yourself. Many men who keep silent are tortured by the fear that, sooner or later, through someone else, in some way they couldn't foresee, they'll be — to put it bluntly — found out."

Davy said, "I told you we didn't exchange full names and neither of us knows where the other lives."

"Still, one or both of you could have learned," Dr. Carstairs said mildly.

"How?" asked Davy, startled.

"The motel register."

Davy's mouth grew hard. He said, "That wouldn't have occurred to me; it would be the last thing I'd *want* to know."

"It might have occurred to her."

He hadn't thought of that.

He said, "I don't believe . . ." Then he looked up and the black eyes were blazing. "I don't know her, of course," he conceded.

"Quite! But it's something you have to consider," said Dr. Carstairs, thereby adding to Davy's burden. This was a new kind of terror. Suppose he walked with Meg, into an unknown house, hotel, restaurant, anywhere in the world; or even into a known one? Suppose he went to a friend's house for an evening or looked across the porch of the country club and saw that red-haired woman sitting there?

"Now," said the minister, watching him, "you're afraid."

"I never thought of that," Davy said dully.

"It's more than unlikely, I think," Dr. Carstairs said, "still, it's within the realm of probability. . . . I've learned over a long lifetime that anything can happen. Just in case it should, it might be better if you told your wife."

Davy thought: Even so, I'm not sure it would be wise . . .

Dr. Carstairs continued, "Your wife loves you, and you love her." He paused and added, "I believe that there is nothing lacking in the physical aspect of your marriage."

It was a question really. Psychiatrists put it differently, but it adds up to the same frame of reference.

"Nothing," Davy answered, and, in a curious sense, felt violated.

"The sex factor of marriage," said Dr. Carstairs, "is also sharing. And if Meg loves you, she will —"

Davy interrupted harshly. He said, "Don't say she'll understand. She won't, and I won't blame her."

"Very well," Carstairs told him, "I won't say it. It's difficult for me to understand, too. What I was going to say is, your wife will be deeply hurt, and this you must face. But you will have shared."

Davy rose. He couldn't stay here a moment longer; the walls were closing in around him He said, "Thanks . . . I'll think it over."

"Shall we —" Dr. Carstairs began and stopped. No. He would not ask: Shall we pray together? Experience had taught him when not to suggest that. He added, "I mean, you'll both be in my prayers, Davy, and I know you'll have guidance. And let me give you a word of advice. If you tell Meg, don't tell her you've confided in me. If she comes to me of her own accord, that's something else again. But don't you tell her."

"I shan't," Davy said.

Tell her this; don't tell her that. He was in a fever to get away, out into the air.

Driving home, he thought: Well, that tears it — if *he* couldn't understand . . .

But Carstairs hadn't said that; he'd said merely that it was difficult for him to understand.

Why should he? How could anyone? Davy

had tried to point out the important, unpardonable fact. . . there was no need. Dr. Carstairs might have understood a sudden drive, a momentary hunger. Men like him were taught to understand that — and some did, with more than their minds, being men. No need whatsoever, and actually, no temptation . . . well, yes, that perhaps for the moment, but not a big, not an overpowering thing.

I won't tell Meg, Davy decided. I'll go on living with myself as best I can. In a month, a few months, a year, I'll have forgotten.

When he came into the house, Meg had a visitor, the new next-door neighbor, who was just about to go. They'd been talking gardens, Meg said, and added, "I've been advising her, probably all wrong. . . . Whatever kept you, Davy? I thought you'd be home long ago and promised Mrs. Sims your really expert advice."

This was a private joke between them. Meg was the gardener, not Davy.

"I ran into someone and we got talking," Davy said, "but I'm ready to advise at all times."

"I'll take you up on that," the neighbor said.

"Did you forget the package from Albert's?" Meg asked.

"No, it's in the hall. You know I never forget," he said, thinking savagely: More's the pity.

"The perfect husband," Mrs. Sims murmured in admiration. "Mine, poor wretch, mails letters for me in town six weeks late. I've learned to put them in the RFD box."

She left, Meg went out to the kitchen, and Davy thought again: I won't tell her.

A few nights later, he did.

CHAPTER 4

It is said that a shock can be cushioned, the bitterest cup sweetened in the pouring. Someone is ill, they say, and when that has been accepted, a word is added. The word is usually "very"; and presently, when the consciousness has again adjusted, the terminal gentle word is spoken.

This was a different kind of death notice.

Meg and Davy were alone in the living room, the windows open to the June night. The coffee cups and service stood on the low, marble-topped table; he hadn't, as yet, taken the tray to the kitchen. And Meg said, moon or no moon rising, the six o'clock news had predicted light rain; and then she asked, "Want to watch TV?"

Davy swallowed. There was an obstruction in his throat. He picked up his cup again and drank what was left of the cooling coffee. He said, "No," and added that he had something to tell her.

She was sitting on one of the love seats across the room from him and she looked at him, her eyes widening with anxiety. The job? she thought. Or, after all the protestations, his health? He hadn't made the appointment with Mike, she knew, although she had continually urged him. Then her glance focused and she saw a face she had never seen: Davy's features, almost unrecognizable with shame, humility, entreaty.

"Davy?"

He lifted his hand and began to speak. His story was quickly told, again without excuses. It had to be recounted in all its naked brevity.

Now he, too, saw an unfamiliar face; struck into white rigidity, then breaking up, as the surface of a pond breaks when the stone is cast; Meg's cheeks became scarlet, and her mouth, square, as in the mask of tragedy.

After that, they spoke to each other in stammered clichés, for in such conversations there is no eloquence.

Meg had never been a jealous woman, but she was an anxious one. There is a difference. She had been married for many years to an unusually attractive man. Women are not drawn only by good looks. She had seen them — friend, acquaintance, stranger — look at Davy with pleasure, with aroused interest, or with swift appraisal. Long ago Amy had warned her, "Women will always be attracted to Davy."

So now and then, at a gathering in her

own or someone else's house, seeing a come-hither glance, overhearing a provocative word, anxiety laid a cold, light finger on her heart. But that was all. Sometimes she spoke of it indirectly, asking, "Mrs. So-and-so is beautiful, don't you think?" and he would answer indifferently, "Yes, I suppose so."

Perhaps most women didn't, actually, want a man attractive to none but themselves, but Meg sometimes did. As a small child, she'd had a doll, battered, almost featureless; it had been discarded by Amy. Meg had other dolls; she exhibited, dressed and undressed them, took them perambulating, sat them at the miniature tea table, tended them with devoted, maternal love. But the battered doll she kept in a little toy chest and always took it to bed with her.

"Why do you want that ugly old thing?" Amy would ask.

"She isn't ugly; she isn't old."

"She's old," contradicted Amy, "and she's ugly. She wasn't ever pretty, not even when she belonged to me."

"She's mine now," Meg said.

The majority of women understand the transient normal reaction of their husbands toward other women. Meg did, also, with her mind. . . . She'd say, "I saw you taking the new blonde into protective custody," and

Davy would retort, "Why not? She's quite a girl." But, if the incident were mentioned again, he would have, quite genuinely, forgotten the girl's name.

Now Meg asked, in a harsh, strangled voice: *"Why?"*

"I don't know," he answered wearily. "There was no reason. I swear it." He tried to tell her, as he'd told Dr. Carstairs, that he could not plead urgency. It was impossible to tell Meg, as it had been to tell the minister, that for a second of time he'd experienced a sort of impersonal compassion . . . the tossed crust, the dime for a cup of coffee, the "Here, will this help?"

No one would believe him; he wondered if he believed himself.

Meg asked, her voice colored by an unmistakable hope: "You were drunk?"

"No," he answered heavily, and meticulously added, for the record, the exact alcoholic intake of that evening: before a substantial dinner, two light Scotches with water; in the motel room one bourbon, with water and ice. Meg knew his capacity and tolerance.

"Then why?" she asked again. "A — a woman you didn't even *know!*"

"For God's sake," he asked — and he was not a man given to profanity — "would you rather it had been someone I — we both — knew?"

She could not answer that or weigh the split hair.

"How could you do this to me?" she demanded and, entirely without volition, began to cry noisily, her face distorted, the tears running over her cheeks and into her open mouth.

Davy rose. It was a long, uphill mile to cover the little space between the love seats. He sat down and tried to take her in his arms. "Meg, don't. Please, don't. . . . Darling — please . . ."

"Don't touch me!"

He moved away from her, and said dully, "All right."

After a while she stopped crying, but she was disfigured with it, the delicate skin blotched, her eyes swollen.

"How could you let this happen to us? How could you do this to me?"

"Meg, it meant nothing, nothing at all."

"Not to you, perhaps," she conceded, yet could not believe it.

People actually do wring their hands, he discovered, for she did so now, a tight, hurting gesture of which she was unaware.

Then she asked piteously, "Why did you tell me, Davy?"

He answered somberly, "I couldn't take it, alone," but did not add: And then I became frightened.

She was ahead of him there. She said, "I'll never go into a new place, or even a place we know, without looking at every strange woman we meet and wondering —"

He couldn't bring himself to admit? "Neither will I." Instead, he said, "Meg, I don't know her name; she doesn't know mine; neither of us knows where the other lives."

Her mind functioned as Dr. Carstairs' had: "You could have found out somehow, from the motel people."

"My God," he said. "It didn't occur to me. I didn't want to know."

Possibly she could accept this, but she went on stubbornly, "She could have —"

"Why? It doesn't make sense."

Nothing made sense to Meg, except: Why wouldn't this woman want to know, whether or not Davy did? That would have made sense to a lot of people.

Corky scratched at the screen door and Davy rose from the corner of the love seat and let him in. The spaniel wandered over to Meg, sat down in front of her, looking up. She did not put her hand on his head or speak to him. Davy was still on his feet and Corky went over to stand close to him.

He was ignored here, too. Something was the matter, something was very wrong. Corky sighed and went to lie down on the cool hearth before the empty fireplace.

"I simply can't believe it of you," Meg said. She'd said it before; she said a number of things several times.

Davy followed Corky to the fireplace, as if for reassurance — a dog's love is uncomplicated.

"I can't either. There's no excuse," he said again. In such moments there is always the endless repetition.

This time Meg answered, "Maybe, if there had been, I could forgive you."

She didn't know whether or not she spoke the truth. And he was incredulous.

"If there'd been an excuse — if — as you mentioned before — I'd been drunk, or fallen in love or was taken with — with this — as with an illness?"

"Perhaps," she said.

She thought: Yes, because that would have made some sense; a little, horrible sense.

She was remembering the Spode pitcher the young child Meg had broken. "I didn't mean to do it, Amy," she had tearfully protested, and the older sister had answered, "That's no excuse." Yet, when she lost her first little ring and explained why she had taken it off her finger and how it must have fallen out of her pocket, that seemed excuse enough for Amy to console her.

"Meg, please listen to me," Davy said and braced himself to go over it all again, and yet again, if necessary.

"What is there to say?"

It went on like that for a long time; desolate question, despairing answer, silence — her hard face broke again into tears, falling, subsiding.

It was late and he was more tired than he'd ever been. "We're not getting anywhere, Meg," he said.

"No."

Where was there to go? At what place could you arrive?

He said mechanically, "Come to bed, dear," and she looked at him with such horror that he was sickened by it.

"I'll take the coffee cups out," she told him, rose, bent her slender body and extended her hands, so lately wrung together, to lift the tray.

He took it from her, without a word, and went to the kitchen. She did not follow him; Corky did, and she heard Davy speak to him lovingly.

She sat down again, small, on the love seat and mentally measured the distance to the hall; she counted the treads of the stairs — fourteen; in her mind she walked up them, opened the door of their bedroom, and went in.

She heard water running; Davy was rinsing the coffee things. She heard the refrigerator door open and close: Davy was putting the cream back in the container.

She rose, stiffly, moved toward the hall and went upstairs. She heard Davy let Corky out. He would go out with him for a while, or wait downstairs — a longer while tonight, she thought. Afterwards, she heard the door close and Davy's voice speaking to the dog; and then the click of a light switch.

Now he was coming upstairs with Corky ahead of him. Their bedroom door stood open; the only light was from the lamp on his bedside table.

He said good night to Corky, turned off the hall light, which also turned one off downstairs, and came in. This was the traditional moment for him to say in the time-honored phrase, "I'll sleep in the guest room tonight." He did not — it was too classic, too fiction, too motion picture, too stage play, too TV — and also too real.

Meg was quiet, lying in her bed. When Davy had undressed, with no word spoken, he turned out his light and found his way across the narrow space between their twin beds; narrow, and as perilous as a deep, unexplored chasm.

He sat down on the edge of her bed. She did not move. He said, "Meg," but he made no attempt to touch her.

"Don't let's talk any more tonight," she said in a voice like that of a tired child.

He rose and went to his own bed. The sheets were cool. The room smelled of early roses, and it was not wholly dark, for moonlight filtered across the floor.

This was their room and he had always loved it; so did Meg; they often told each other they'd bought this house for the big bedroom.

Tonight they lay awake, each in his own cell. And when he heard her crying again, he got up and went to her. He tried, this time, to take her in his arms and felt her repudiation.

"Let me get you a sleeping pill, Meg?"

"No. I'm sorry to keep you awake," she said, once more in the voice of a child, a good child.

He returned again to his bed and lay looking up at the ceiling, his arms behind his head.

How did he feel? He did not wholly know. He knew he felt pain; he knew he felt unconquerable hope. It can't go on like this, he told himself. Tomorrow — or if not tomorrow, another day, someday — things will come right again. He knew he felt both burdened and light . . . light, because he was no longer alone with his guilt.

He slept at last, to be awakened by Meg's weeping, muted now but relentless. The room was cool with the paling night and it was raining, a quiet rain and beneficent. In an hour or two it would probably cease.

The light in the room was gray and he rose wearily, unrefreshed and anxious, and took the few necessary steps toward Meg's bed. She was not fully awake, for he heard her say, "Amy?" in a faint, forlorn voice. When he sat down and once more put his arms about her, she did not draw away; the earlier rigidity was gone; she was soft and warm from sleep, and vulnerable. She began to cry against him, waking now, remembering, but too unhappy to deny herself the familiar strength of the arms around her.

"Darling . . ."

She whimpered, catching her breath, but did not answer.

"Meg?" He felt tears on his cheeks, but they were not hers. "Meg, try, please try to forgive me."

She said, "No." She said, "I can't," yet

moved her head against him as if in acquiescence and drifted back to sleep.

Davy put her down against the pillows, and left her. He could visualize her waking later in the morning and finding him beside her, and he could not face what he would see in her opening eyes. He went noiselessly to his own bed and waited for the new day, which always comes.

He fell briefly asleep just before the rain stopped and the birds that had been talking softly to one another, it seemed for hours, began to sing. As he woke, he knew the moment of split consciousness: it is morning, everything is normal; then you remember. It is like this the morning after a death, and for many mornings thereafter.

He sat up slowly. Meg was not in her bed; she was not in the room. He came to his feet, feeling the impact of the floor in something close to panic. He had not heard her go.

Someone was moving about downstairs, and he heard Corky barking. He thought inconsequently: What day is it?

Doomsday — and Mrs. Lowry's.

When he was dressed, Corky came upstairs to take him to breakfast. The dining table was set; he smelled coffee. Meg was in the kitchen, where they usually had breakfast in pleasant intimacy.

Her eyes were still swollen and there was no color in her face, except where she had put it unevenly on her lips.

Do you say, "Good morning," do you say, "Hi"?

He said awkwardly, "I didn't hear you leave the room."

"I took my things into the guest room," she answered. "You were asleep."

Did he imagine a reproach? Yet she, too, had slept.

"Can I help you?"

"No, thanks."

But he took the tray from her and carried it to the table. The good coffee was scalding; he drank it black and burned his mouth. Meg drank hers and crumbled toast, while Davy looked at the bland, white and yellow face of the egg on his plate and forced himself to eat. He said aloud, "You have to eat something," and whether he spoke to himself or her, he didn't know. But she answered, "I'm not hungry."

So the morning's routine began, except that it was not quite as usual. She did not come out to his car with him before getting into her own to go for Mrs. Lowry. He could imagine their conversation:

"You all right, Mrs. Jones? You don't look so good."

"I'm fine, thanks, Mrs. Lowry."

"Got a cold? Your eyes are swollen."

"It's an allergy, I think."

Yes, something like that. Mrs. Lowry took a personal interest in her people.

When he was leaving, with Corky barking farewell, Meg called from the doorway, "Will you be home for lunch?"

"I don't think so. . . . No," he said definitely, "I have things to catch up on."

She turned, went inside the house, and closed the door. He felt that, in her heart, she locked it, and an unreasoning anger began to build up in him.

It was like that for several days. They ate breakfast and dinner together. They kept their engagements, except on the night they were to go to the Watsons. Then Meg said she had a headache. He knew she could not endure an evening of the Watsons and vacation plans.

Now and then they talked: roses, the grass, the weather, the canker in Corky's ear — Meg would take him to the vet's — the mail, if it held mutual interest. Once, when he came home for a report he'd forgotten, he found her standing by the mailbox, the carrier having just left. She was looking at the envelopes with an almost fierce concentration.

If she expected Vivian — was that her name? — to write, it was more than he did, yet it put the insane possibility into his mind. What if she had asked for his address casually? What if she were to write?

No, that wouldn't happen.

Sometimes the delicate surface cracked, and it all boiled up again; it was as if they walked in a seismic country and did not know when the ground would open beneath their feet.

Often she forced him back to the beginning, to the futile retracing, but not always. At least once he began it: "Meg, let's talk. We've got to be sensible about this."

"Sensible?" she repeated, and startled him by laughing. Then she said, "I'd rather not discuss it."

"But we must."

"There's nothing to discuss."

No, nothing that hadn't been said.

Or perhaps she'd begin it, "Why, Davy, why?" and once she remarked, "You were always such a fastidious man."

That was true enough. He did not answer.

Sometimes they spoke of love and those were the worst times of all.

"But I love you, Meg. I've always loved you, always."

"You never loved me." She knew this was

not so, but it always has to be said. "If you loved me, you couldn't have done this to me."

One morning, at breakfast, she said abruptly, "I've called Amy. I'm going there today."

He felt an extraordinary relief, a flash, instantly gone, and then, fear. He asked, humiliated to his very spirit, "You intend to tell Amy?"

"I haven't anyone else."

It was true; she had innumerable friends, some of whom she loved, with whom she laughed, worked, spoke and shared; but she, too, was a fastidious person. She would not confide in them, not even in Helen Watson.

He said, "Meg . . . this is just between us."

"You had to tell," she reminded him. "You had to share it."

He was silent, thinking of Dr. Carstairs.

After a while he asked how long she'd be gone and she said a few days; she didn't know how many. A taxi could fetch and carry Mrs. Lowry. She spoke of the laundry man's day. She said Corky should go once more to the doctor's. Everything was organized. He could go out for dinner, or stay home; there was plenty in the freezer.

He thought of the times when she'd been

ill or tired, or when, just for fun, he had cooked their dinner. She often said he was almost as good a cook as she, but with more imagination. When they invited more people than Meg thought she could handle, they hired the couple all the neighborhood used to cook and serve. He thought how often he'd said, "But we can afford someone regularly now," and she'd answered, "I like it this way."

Now he nodded. Whether he went out or stayed in was a matter of indifference to them both.

She said that if he didn't need the station wagon, she'd leave it at the garage near the railroad; she was going by train. Amy lived in New Jersey.

Driving to the office, knowing that he would return to a house empty except for Corky — but no emptier than it had been in the past week — it occurred to Davy that, as far as the distance between them was concerned, Meg might have been setting out on a journey to Tibet.

CHAPTER 5

In the smoky, sultry train Meg sat next to a woman with innumerable packages. Perhaps, Meg thought, folding her gloved hands and closing her eyes, this flight was a mistake, for henceforth, between her husband and her sister there would be, at best, an armed truce. She tried to evaluate their relationship over the past fourteen years. Amy had always acknowledged Davy's charm, and praised what she called his essential character. She was, she said often, very fond of him. And Davy admired his sister-in-law openly but, Meg thought, with reservations. Once, when he and Meg had a small quarrel over an invitation to New Jersey, which he hadn't wanted to accept, he had remarked that, as much as he liked Amy, she sometimes seemed to him — especially when he was tired — like a velvet steam roller.

Meg remembered that when, long ago, she had told her sister of her engagement, Amy had kissed her, wished her happiness, and remarked that Davy wouldn't have been her selection for Meg, but, of course, since they loved each other, she was pleased for them.

Amy had backed several candidates who came to see Meg, either at their father's house or Amy's. These were solid, ambitious, affable boys, of alleged good families and each with a predictably good future. Amy herself was conditioned to futures, having married a man whose future had been assured by his parents. She lived with Edwin Mason in outward comfort and, at two-year intervals, had produced three healthy children without, apparently, the slightest inconvenience.

I must talk to Amy, Meg thought. But why? It was not advice she wanted. She did not for a moment entertain the thought of leaving her husband. Hence, she could not ask Amy: Shall I stay with him, or leave him? Meg believed in the marriage vows. She had promised Davy — standing at an altar in a church full of music, white flowers, and people — that until death did them part she would be his wife.

What, then, did she want of Amy?

It was warm on the train, which offered a temperamental air-conditioning system, but Meg shivered. If Davy had — instead — died?

If Davy had died, she could have held to the ideal and preserved the image. There would have been no flaw. If Davy had died, her life would have ended, no matter how long thereafter she physically lived.

One of us must die first, her mind told her.

She had occasionally considered this when someone they knew had dropped dead of a coronary, or been killed in an accident, or taken off by something the antibiotics could not reach. Every time she read or heard of such a disaster, she thought, tremulous: Suppose it had been Davy? And this preceded her natural sympathy for the man's wife and children and momentarily blotted out the sun of her own serene life.

Take me first, she would pray silently, laying a paper aside or replacing a telephone receiver. Take me first. . . .

When she reached her station, she picked up her suitcase and the conductor helped her off the train. He had an eye for a trim figure, a slim ankle, and a pretty, if somewhat abstracted, smile.

Meg took a cab to Amy's house, which was a short way out of town and, like Amy, handsome, gracious, and impressive. It was not a house of which one said, "How pretty," or "How charming," or "How quaint." They didn't say that of Amy, either. The house — and Amy — had been photographed for the magazines even more often than the plant in which Davy worked.

It was about five years old, and Amy had presided over its building from the first sketch on the drawing board. Much of the furniture had come from the house in which Amy and her husband had formerly lived and which they had sold at a profit. Some of the things Edwin had inherited from his parents. Some they had bought. Edwin, even more than his wife, had unerring instinct and taste for fine furniture and paintings. He owned some valuable art. He was a man of considerable means through inheritance, his own astute operations on Wall Street, and the substantial business in which he was a senior partner.

The taxi swooped up the curving blacktop driveway and Meg saw the familiar setting: the pool reflecting bending trees, the walled rose garden, and the simple structure of the big house, as beautifully proportioned as its mistress, who came out to the steps and waved as Meg stood paying the driver.

Amy was taller than Meg and resembled her only in coloring, but Amy's hair was a darker gold, with less red, and she'd never cut it. Over her left temple there was a streak of pure silver; she'd had it since girlhood.

Amy Mason was forty-four years old, and almost everyone liked her. She managed, without seeming to, many of the community interests. Some of the women on her committees loved her; a few viewed her through the gentle mist of adoration. She was kind, practical, and responsible; also, just. She did not expect of anyone more work than she herself was willing to do. No one could remotely imagine her awkward, at a loss or, in any situation, embarrassed.

The cab drove away and Amy came down the steps. She kissed her sister's cheek. "Let me take your bag," she said.

"It's light."

"You've had quite a trip and it's unreasonably warm. You look tired. Here, let me . . ."

She was strong. She never had headaches; she said she was the only woman she knew whose feet or back didn't hurt her. She played tennis and golf, swam well, walked, knocked croquet balls around, and openly deplored Meg's tendency to avoid exercise except in a garden. "Why didn't you drive out?" she asked.

"I didn't feel like it, Amy."

Davy hadn't asked her why she wasn't driving; he'd lifted an eyebrow but made no comment. The simple truth was she'd been afraid to drive, frightened by the confusion of her thoughts and emotional reactions.

"How peaceful it looks," she said as they went up the steps. A maid materialized, spoke, smiling, to Meg, and took her suitcase.

"It is now," Amy agreed. "The children aren't home yet. After they come, it will be bedlam as usual. They have all sorts of summer plans. Are you going to Vermont again?"

"I suppose so," Meg said as they started up the curving staircase.

"Habit's a curious thing. I'd think you'd get tired of it. . . . Let me know the dates; Edwin and I might run up and stay at the Lodge."

They were on the wide landing when Amy said, "I hope you won't mind being in the single room in this wing; the other's been painted and isn't back together yet."

Meg didn't mind; quite the contrary, because when she and Davy visited here, they shared the double guest room.

The single room was ample, subdued in coloring, except for a brilliant flash of tangerine in the cushions on the chaise longue . . . muted grays, greens, and the tangerine. It was a pleasant room.

Amy walked about, drawing her finger across a night table and the bureau and then looking at it. She was a tireless housekeeper.

She sat on the edge of the chaise as Meg began to unpack. The clothes closet and bureau drawers, unlike those of most guest rooms, were empty, the padded hangers and the satin lining of the drawers faintly scented.

Meg vanished into the bathroom which opened from the room and was part of it; she murmured over her shoulder, ". . . terribly dusty train ride . . ."

Amy said, "Why on earth didn't you tell me what train you were taking so I could meet you?"

She rose to smooth the counterpane and then returned to the chaise; she never sat on beds.

Meg emerged from the bathroom, rubbing her hands together, "I like your new hand lotion," she said and then answered, "I'd lost the timetable, so I just took the first train I could make to New York and waited for the next one out here."

"You're thin," Amy remarked.

"No more than usual . . . it's this dress," Meg said, indicating the dark, two-piece cotton. She took comb, brush, and cosmetic case from her bag and sat at the dressing table. There were Spartan roses on it, in a slender vase.

Amy watched her sister brush her pretty

hair, short and soft. The deep wave across the top of her small head was natural.

"How's Davy?"

"He's just fine. Corky, too."

Amy said. "Good," and thought: Why is she here, out of the blue? What's happened?

Reason was stronger in her than intuition; reason explained her husband to her, her children and friends, and also Meg, who was not given to telephoning and asking in a tight, hurried voice, "Are you terribly busy? . . . May I come out for a few days?"

She and Davy must have quarreled, thought Amy.

Meg hadn't come looking for consolation since the first year of her marriage. During that year she had asked, frequently, the usual questions! "How? . . . Why? . . . What am I to do?" Like Meg, Amy had been married at twenty and it had always seemed to the younger sister, since she'd been able to evaluate anything at all, that Amy knew all the answers. So the little girl who'd always asked, "How? . . . Why? . . . What shall I do?" went on asking for a time, but not for long. After the shakedown cruise, she'd developed, as it were, a strong sense of loyalty to the ship.

She had continued to solicit her sister's advice in matters not pertaining directly to her marriage: house, clothes, situations in the neighborhood — Amy knew all about community problems — or misunderstandings with friends.

"It's early," Amy remarked, looking at a small gold clock on the night table, "but let's have tea in the garden. Edwin won't be home for dinner; he asked me this morning to say he was sorry. You'll be in bed when he gets back; you'd better be, you look tired . . . why don't you change your dress?"

"I've just done my hair."

"You can do it over; besides you unbutton . . . there's something about that dress . . . I want to see if you really look as bushed as when you came in."

So Meg unbuttoned, put on a bright silk print, which also fastened down the front, and not a hair of her head was disturbed.

Then they had tea in the rose garden. They talked about people and things, about Amy's children: the boys, Edwin, Jr., and Marty, in college; the girl, Hilary, away at school. "All sorts of goings on," said Amy. "Hilary's gone to Ohio for her roommate's debut and rounds of parties. The boys both have projects before they descend upon us."

She was proud of her children. They looked like her and rarely, except for occasional illnesses, caused her any anxiety. She worried only lest they marry unwisely despite her concealed training . . . at least, she believed it concealed. But marriages were a long way off. Hilary would make her debut in the autumn, graduate a year from now and go on to what is known as higher education, probably — if the world situation did not worsen — in Europe. The junior Edwin had been deferred from the armed forces until graduation, and his younger brother had two years to go. "Two graduations next June," said Amy, "Ed's and Hilary's. I don't know how we can be in two places at once."

"Perhaps they won't be on the same date," Meg said, watching a bee dart about the roses. Her voice was colorless.

Amy thought: Well, she'll tell me what's wrong in her own time.

Meg roused herself to speak of their stepmother who, since their father's death, had lived in California, and to ask if Amy had heard from their half brother and sister.

Then, she said, "You're always so busy . . . I hope I haven't upset your plans, barging in like this with practically no notice."

"No . . . the Carmens are coming to dinner tomorrow night — you've met them — and such outside engagements as I had were simple to cancel. None was important. I do serve a hitch at the Thrift Shop tomorrow;

you can come along and watch the customers fight, or, if you'd rather, stay home and rest."

The whole house was conducive to rest — the living room and library, Amy's morning room, Edwin's study. Even the big dining room lent itself to unheated discussion. The children had their own wing, built to accommodate them and their guests. Amy and Edwin had a suite: bedroom, two dressing rooms and a bath, somewhat removed from the guest rooms. The house ran in silent order. Amy had a genius for employing the right people and, since she was just, if firm, and the wages high, she rarely was forced to replace anyone.

Now she'd have to, she told Meg, sighing. It appeared that Matilda, the maid who had cheerfully carried Meg's suitcase, was going to be married.

"And I just had her trained," Amy deplored. "Such a nice girl. The boy, I think, is unsuitable."

Over what you might call a broad spectrum, all marriages to Amy were either suitable or unsuitable.

After a moment she put down her glass; the ice tinkled, the fresh mint dispensed its fragrance. "You can't tell me you came this distance just to chat?"

"No," Meg admitted, her pulse accelerating.

"Money?" asked Amy briskly. Not that Davy wasn't doing well enough, but the unexpected often happens. She turned over the possibilities in her mind. The mortgage had been paid, she knew; there'd been no sudden illness; there were no children for whom expensive trips, school, riding, dancing and other lessons must be provided. She thought of the stock market. She knew Davy's broker slightly; a conservative man Edwin had recommended. However, she thought, Davy had always been given to flights of fancy.

Meg was speaking. "No, it isn't money, I'd rather we talked later, Amy," she said.

"All right, dear," her sister agreed comfortably.

When they went into the house, Amy suggested that Meg undress, really undress, and lie down. "Drinks at six-thirty," she said briskly; "then, dinner. I've some phoning to do, and you won't be disturbed."

Up in the single guest room they stood a moment looking at each other and Amy bent to kiss Meg's forehead. She was restrained in demonstration, but the protective love was always there.

Amy went downstairs into the morning room, bright with hand-blocked linen, gay with plants, and sat down at an antique desk. Most of the furniture in this house was of an older, more formal period than Meg's charming, haphazard, early, or middle, American and Victorian.

Drawing the telephone toward her, Amy frowned. If it wasn't money, she thought, or a possibility of Davy's losing his job . . . Had he lost it? No that wouldn't happen; he was a valuable man. It had to be women or a specific woman. . . . Not Meg, never Meg, she assured herself.

She dialed a member of one of her committees, thinking: It narrows down to Davy. . . . I could have sworn — but who can fathom any man?

Upstairs, Meg lay on the single bed and tried not to cry. She had believed that all the tears were shed, and she was empty of them, yet at unexpected moments they rose to her eyes or solidified into a knot in her throat . . . when she wasn't even thinking, she told herself drearily, when she was just talking to someone in a supermarket, or walking outside, or bringing Corky home from the vet's.

If she cried, Amy would notice; she'd never been able to conceal tears from Amy. It had been:

"Amy, my doll's broken. . . . Amy, I fell

and cut my knee. . . . Amy, it's raining and we can't have the picnic. . . . Amy, I was sent to the principal's office."

And Amy would say, "I'll fix your doll . . . I'll bandage your knee. . . . We'll have the picnic on the screened porch. . . . I'll talk to your teacher."

At eighteen, Amy had successfully talked to Meg's teacher, but now . . . Sooner or later, Meg thought, I suppose I'll cry.

There was no answer when Amy tapped on her sister's door about six-thirty, so she went in and found Meg sleeping. She went quietly to the bed and looked down. Meg's hands were balled into little fists, and she'd tossed a pillow to the floor. Amy's heart constricted. . . . Meg looked so young, so very young. But, then, she had always looked young.

Amy thought: She's been crying; I thought so, when she came. Not that Meg's eyes were swollen, but the lids looked stained, and the fine skin beneath the eyes, almost bruised.

If he's hurt her . . . thought Amy.

"Meg?" she said.

Meg stirred, opened her eyes, blinked for a moment, as if with confusion. Then she sat up and said, "I didn't mean to sleep."

"Well, you did and it was good for you."

Amy stooped to retrieve the pillow. "Do you have lounging pajamas with you? . . . No? I'd lend you a pair of mine, but you'd swim in them."

"I brought slacks."

"They'll do. We may as well be comfortable for dinner," Amy said. She herself was wearing the straight trousers and coat of dark brocade that she'd bought in Hong Kong.

In the living room, massed with flowers — "Too many," Amy commented. "I meant to speak to Gibbons. The place looks like a funeral parlor" — they had aperitifs. The little bar was so constructed that the panels above it slid open. Given her choice of drinks, Meg selected a Martini and, to Amy's troubled astonishment, drank three, although she usually confined herself to one, two at the most.

A deft waitress made the drinks; Edwin had taught her.

For a while the Masons had gone in for experienced butlers, but Amy had grown impatient with them. She sometimes woke at night and went prowling downstairs to the refrigerator or her desk. She was almost always hungry; her energy seemed to demand quantities of food, but she restrained herself and was never overweight. Often, when she lay awake, she thought of the letter she hadn't written, the check she hadn't drawn. Edwin was accustomed to her departures and rarely even woke. But going into the kitchen, or morning room, and encountering a butler — they, too, seemed unable to sleep — unnerved her, Amy decided, so now the house was run by a competent staff of women, and the male employees functioned in the grounds and garage.

The dining room was immense; the big table seated twenty — more if necessary, with extra leaves. But a smaller table was set by the French doors which opened onto the terrace. "I thought we'd eat outside," Amy said, "but it's turned a little cool and although everything's been sprayed, we have the usual unwelcome visitors flying about. . . . Meg, for heaven's sake, eat something."

In this room Edwin's formidable ancestors regarded, without interest, the occupants, the excellent food, the carafe of *vin rosé*. The big oval table in the middle of the room reflected, in shining wood, a footed silver bowl of roses.

Afterward, coffee on the terrace. "We'll chance it," said Amy. "Here's a sweater."

Later they walked around the gardens, and for a while they sat in the long chairs and watched the light fade until Amy slapped at a mosquito.

"I told you so," she said with resignation. "Those special candles in the hurricane lamps don't discourage them. Let's go in."

In the house Meg asked, a little timidly, "May I go to bed now?" much as she used to ask, "*Must* I go to bed?"

"Of course. . . . There are things to read, I put a couple of good books on the night table. There's a sleeping pill in the Sèvres cup just in case, and Matilda will have brought your water thermos."

So, thought Amy, not tonight.

In bed, Meg fought against the need to go down the hall and cross the corridor to where Amy was, presumably reading in bed as was her habit, and to creep in beside her and say, "Amy, I'm so miserable. . . . How could he do this to me?" Once the urge seemed unconquerable, and she sat up and swung her slender legs over the edge of the bed; but at that moment she heard a car drive up and knew Edwin had returned home.

She turned on the light and took the sleeping pill, although she detested the idea. She almost choked on the small capsule remembering: "Let me get you a sleeping pill,

Meg?" Then she switched off the light again and put her head on the scented pillow.

"Edwin had to get off early," Amy reported the next morning, coming into Meg's room, opening the curtains and pulling up the shades to full sunlight. "He sends his love. . . . Don't get up."

"I meant to."

"Just as well you didn't — it was gulp and rush. Matilda will bring you a tray. How about bacon and eggs?"

"Just coffee," said Meg faintly. "I'm sorry I didn't see Edwin."

"You will tonight. And not just coffee. . . . Fruit, toast, and marmalade. Did you sleep?"

"Oh, yes."

Amy regarded her with satisfaction; she did look rested. Then she vanished and presently the tray was brought in.

That was a long day; and busy. Meg went out to the gardens with Amy, who wanted to talk to Gibbons, the gardener — there was some dissatisfaction with his helper. They inspected Edwin's elegant new car — he took his old one to the station and left it there. And after a while they went driving in Amy's convertible, so Meg could be shown what had happened to the countryside since last she had seen it — which had been in March. They stopped in town to lunch in a pleasant place, where every other woman who came in knew Amy, and then they went to the Thrift Shop, where Meg watched and waited until Amy had accomplished over two hours of barter.

Edwin came home early, glad to see his sister-in-law, asking about Davy. "Why didn't you bring him? I haven't seen him — or you — for too long. Last time I saw him was weeks ago when we had lunch together."

Edwin was very little taller than Amy and had put on weight recently, but he still looked somewhat younger than he was. He was a kind, clever man, and Meg was fond of him.

She knew the dinner guests, the Carmens, slightly and after coffee they played contract. . . . At Amy's insistence Meg sat in for a couple of rubbers, once when Amy was out of the game, on the telephone, and again when Mr. Carmen said he wanted to take a breather on the terrace.

"Only thing you lack, Edwin," he told his host, "is a dog — a couple of dogs."

Amy could take dogs or leave them. She enjoyed dog shows, and admired the noble look of champions and when Meg was little, Amy had persuaded her father to let the younger girl have a puppy. But the only dog Amy and Edwin had owned, when they were first married, had lived to be eleven and then was killed by a car. He had been more Edwin's dog than Amy's, but she had grieved for him, as had the children. She explained to them that there would be no other dog, for, as they grew up, they'd be away much of the time and could not then fulfill their responsibilities toward an animal; and she didn't wish to substitute.

After the Carmens left, Meg sat awhile in the library, where Edwin was having a nightcap. She'd refused one. She'd been abstentious before, and after, dinner, but her head ached just as much as it had last night, when she'd ascribed it to the Martinis. Edwin asked questions, told a joke or two, launched into a business discussion with his wife, "Better business head on her shoulders than my partners," he often said, and, finally, they all went upstairs.

A long day, Meg thought. What had Davy been doing since she left?

CHAPTER 6

What he was doing was marking time, not daring to go forward or backward. How long would Meg be gone? he wondered. Would she ever return? And he did not mean: Would she come driving up from the station garage and open her own front door?

Fortunately, at the office, minor problems arose which required his attention, and he worked late the first two nights of Meg's absence, going out to a hurried dinner, then returning to his desk. At night the office had an eerie quality; there were few people there: night watchmen making rounds, cleaning women, and two men in the accounting department, also putting in overtime.

On the second day he went to see Dr. Miller. Urged by Meg, bombarded with telephone calls from Miller's secretary, he'd finally made the appointment.

In the pleasant offices he submitted to the examination, including an EKG.

"You're in good shape," said Mike, "barring some tension. How astonished I'd be if I had a patient over say, twelve, who didn't have tension. . . . What about your pet pain?"

"Only when I eat or drink what I shouldn't, or too much."

"Sleeping well?"

"Not very."

"I'll give you something for that."

"I still have some capsules from the last time," Davy said.

Mike consulted Davy's folder. He said, "Oh. Take 'em for a while; they won't hurt you. Meg's worried about you, Davy."

"She is?" Davy asked evenly.

"Must be. . . . She backed me into a corner at the Clinic, a few weeks ago, and asked if you'd been to see me. She was very casual about it, of course. Tell her not to fret, will you? I think you'll live to be ninety-nine."

"I have already."

"Oh, so it's like that, is it?" Mike inquired.

"Just like that."

"*Weltschmerz,*" the doctor diagnosed. "It afflicts us all from time to time. It's hard not to age rapidly in a world which is jumping and jumpy. Any special personal reason for your sense of having become venerable?"

"Nope," Davy answered, "and since spring's over — just about — it can't be spring fever."

"What you need is a vacation."

"I bet you say that to all your patients."

"I do; and also to myself. Or Ginger does.

Which reminds me, I told Meg that Ginger would call her. I forgot to tell Ginger, naturally, but I shall; we ought to get together more outside this office."

"Fine," said Davy. He added, "Meg's gone to her sister's for a few days."

"Oh? Nice woman, Meg's sister. . . . What's her name again?"

"Amy . . . Amy Mason."

"She scares me a little," Mike admitted, "but I like her. Well, when Meg gets back, we'll have a date." He pressed the button which would summon the next patient, and Davy rose. "Look," said Mike, "simmer down, boy . . . take up gardening or knitting — it's very fashionable in England — or play more golf."

"Galloping blood pressure?" Davy inquired, without interest, and Mike said, "No, or I would have told you. Oh, sure, a little rise, but nothing to be alarmed about and not, I'm certain, organic. Just tension. . . . Take it easy, Davy."

He tried — on the links, for instance, and out to dinner with one of his associates, also a temporary bachelor. At the office he was too busy to think much, and he tried to be too tired at night; he didn't succeed, but the sleeping pill helped. Bob Watson called him relative to the Vermont holiday; they'd renewed their lease early in the winter and they talked dates, fishing, and probable weather. "How you fixed for money?" Bob asked. "I'm saving against the usual catastrophes. Now, if only we could find one country road without an antique shop on it . . ."

Davy laughed because it was expected of him. Bob said that, one way or another, every year, and Davy had always laughed.

He was, at this time, harder to work with than usual; he drove others, and he also drove himself. Sometimes he was even a little short with Corky, whose feelings he thereby wounded.

What was Meg doing? What was she saying? . . . She had not once telephoned him as she always did when she went away. Had she told Amy? . . . Of course she had, he thought.

She told her, on the third evening when, after dinner they'd vanished onto the terrace because one of the town's political figures came to consult Edwin.

"Let's go upstairs," Meg said restlessly and Amy looked at her, thinking: Here it comes.

They went up to Amy's bedroom, one end of which was slightly raised to make a living room, with comfortable chairs, a fireplace, a table where two could breakfast, and photographs of the children all around; over the fireplace, a portrait of them, in pastels, done some years ago when they were small.

Meg walked around nervously. She took a silver-framed picture from a table, looked at it, and put it down without comment. Then she said, "I think I'll go home early tomorrow."

"Without telling me why you came?" Amy asked.

"No," she answered. And then, still standing, told her a little astonished that the matter could be so briefly and baldly stated.

Amy sat still, not interrupting. She was startled, disgusted, and incredulous; she was also weak with pity for the younger woman, but within herself, somewhat impatient.

"Margaret," she said, and she rarely called her sister that, "I'm so sorry —"

"Yes, I know. So am I," said Meg with bitterness.

"Do sit down," Amy said and when Meg obediently sat, she asked, "Must you take this so seriously?"

"How else can I take it?" Meg demanded.

"Dear —" Amy hesitated, for this was a difficult situation — "just with a grain of common sense. . . . Mind you, I don't understand Davy, and I doubt if he understands himself. . . . I certainly don't dismiss or condone it; still, it's happened. . . . I don't know how to say this, really, but — it's just that it didn't *mean* anything."

"He said that, too," Meg told her stonily.

"I'm sure he was telling you the truth. Look, Meg, suppose it had meant something. Suppose it had been someone you both knew —"

"He also said that."

"— and had been going on for a long time," Amy went on, without commenting on the interruption. "That would have been serious. This isn't."

"Maybe I'm very stupid," Meg said, "but I think it's serious. I think it's unpardonable."

After a moment Amy said, "I'm older than you, Meg, and I've seen far worse breaches mended." She frowned and was silent for a little as if she were searching in the files for a case history. "For instance — Edwin and I knew a couple before we moved here. You've met them, so I won't put labels on them. They'd been married for some time when it started — very discreetly. But she found out . . . it was someone she trusted, someone often in their house."

Meg asked, not really caring, "What did she do?"

"Waited," Amy answered. "She knew it wouldn't last. They had a good marriage and children. She realized it was an infatuation."

"How does anyone really know that?"

"Well, let's say, she counted on it's being one. No one in the community knew, I believe, except me. She talked to me about it," Amy said, and Meg could believe that. Everyone came to Amy for advice. "She told me she wasn't going to ruin her own life and unsettle the children's."

"But suppose it had turned out not to be an infatuation?"

"She wouldn't have given him a divorce, no matter how much he wanted one."

"Did he?"

"He thought so, but not for long."

"How could she go back to him?" Meg asked.

"I know this sounds very reactionary," Amy answered. "Even Hilary would laugh if she could hear me — but she believed it was her duty."

Amy was a champion of duty and Meg thought, appalled: She's really talking about herself and Edwin. . . . *Edwin?* . . . It's incredible. I mustn't let her know — she'd never tell me outright — she has too much pride.

For the first time in her life, Meg saw her sister as vulnerable.

She said, "But this hasn't anything to do with me, Amy. I — I could understand that better, somehow. This," she went on in a terrible voice, the more terrible because it was so quiet, "is without any excuse at all, even that of infatuation."

Amy thought: I could murder Davy. She was sure she would never condone his — what was it exactly? Lapse? Lunacy? Whatever it was, she couldn't understand it, but Meg must be led to see that, understanding or not, she could not permit her life to be destroyed. She rose, went across to Meg's chair, drew her to her feet. "Why don't you cry, Margaret?" she asked.

"I thought I would, when I was with you. But I can't. I've been crying so much." She put her head on Amy's shoulder. "I'm so unhappy," she said.

"I know, dear; I know."

After a while, Meg drew away and stood like a child, her hands folded. She said, "I didn't want to upset you, Amy, but I had to tell you."

"Meg, do you want me to advise you what to do?"

"I don't know," Meg said.

"You know what I'd advise, don't you?"

"Yes. You'd say, 'Go home and forgive him.' "

"What else is there to do," asked Amy, "when you strip it down to essentials?"

Meg said, "I don't know. . . . I think I'll take a morning train, Amy."

It was Amy who cried — later, when she was alone — with pity and frustration, with bewilderment and the ripping open of old wounds she had believed healed.

Meg went home, traveling in a dusty train, changing to another, taking cabs. Amy had driven her to the station and, when they kissed each other good-by, said, "Come back if you want to; write me when you can," and added inadequately, "I'll be thinking of you."

She would also, Meg knew, pray for her.

"Futile journey," the car wheels said, creaking, "futile journey."

When Meg reached her station, she went across to the garage, got into her car and drove home. Once she was inside the house, she dropped her suitcase on the floor and looked at the time; it was just past noon.

She called the office and asked for Mrs. Easton, Davy's secretary, and politely inquired if she would please tell Mr. Jones that Mrs. Jones was now home.

She was upstairs unpacking, with Corky

galloping about her, when the telephone rang, and it sounded louder than any bell she'd ever heard.

"Yes?" she answered.

"Meg . . . ?"

"Hello, Davy," Meg said. "Is it too late or do you want to come home for lunch?"

"I have to lunch with one of the engineers who is in from the Coast. I didn't know you'd be home."

"That's all right," she said, aware of relief at the brief postponement. "I'll expect you for dinner."

"Let's go out," he said instantly, thinking what it would be like going home to dinner. "You must be tired. Forget the kitchen. Suppose we go to the Club?"

"All right," she said indifferently and hung up, thinking — accurately: He doesn't want to come home. He wants to be where there are other people. Perhaps I do, too.

She made herself a sandwich and coffee and, sitting at the kitchen table, looking out on a bright, green world, she prayed. At least she believed she was praying; she hadn't for some time; there seemed no one to appeal to except, of course, Amy, and Amy hadn't answered her pleas.

How could she? Meg thought. What did I expect her to do? Cry over me? Send a firing squad after Davy? Take me to Europe or off on a cruise?

No; she had to make up her own mind and she was not accustomed to doing that except in the ordinary situations which involved Mrs. Lowry, or the butcher, or committees or daytime invitations which did not include Davy.

That wasn't strictly true. She decided on colors and clothes and curtains and furniture . . . except when the bill would come high and then she asked, "Can we afford it?"

All her life she had had someone to lean on, first Amy and then Davy. She could no longer lean on either of them, she told herself drearily. Not that Amy had failed her, unless, of course, she'd expected a miracle — and perhaps she had — but apparently she'd outgrown Amy. Now she would have to lean on herself, and she did not know how.

When Davy came in, Meg met him, summoned by Corky and the sound of the car. She saw at once that he did not know what to say, that he wished to kiss her but was afraid, and she did not want to be kissed. But she sliced the loaf in half, offered him her cheek, and said, "I'm all ready; you go upstairs and shave and change."

He said, "I'm glad you're home. I phoned

for a table. . . . I won't be long."

While he was upstairs, she stood looking out the front window, and found that she was breathing as rapidly and heavily as if she had run the mile — or, for her life.

Davy took his time about shaving and dressing, wondering meanwhile: Had Meg in any way altered? What had she decided, or rather into what course of action — or nonaction — had Amy persuaded her docile sister?

He was angry, illogically, at Amy.

After a while he came downstairs. They consoled and admonished Corky — "We'll be home soon. Watch the house, and be a good boy" — got into Davy's car, which he'd left in the driveway, and went to the Club.

It was fairly crowded, which was usual on Friday nights. They saw people they knew, joined the Warings at the bar and, as they entered the dining room, encountered the Watsons. So the captain was called and arrangements made for a table for four. The conversation was, as usual, easy, familiar: "Did you have fun at Amy's or did she work you to death?" And then, of course, talk of Vermont in August. By then, said Helen Watson hopefully, their youngest could have caught and recovered from the measles which were going the rounds.

It was not dance night at the Club, for which Meg was grateful; she had always loved to dance with Davy.

When they'd had coffee, the Joneses made no move to go home, but the Watsons did.

"Tomorrow's Saturday," Davy reminded them. "Live it up."

"Sure, it's always Saturday after Friday except when you cross the international date line," Bob agreed. "I'll see you on the links and beat hell out of you, Davy, if I survive the night. Just now I feel as if someone had beaten hell out of me. I had to attend a special hearing and it took approximately twenty years. . . . Helen, drag me out of this den of vice and put me to bed because I'm to be Queen of the May."

So they all went home.

Davy took Corky for a run, and was gone some time. Meg hesitated: Should she wait? Should she go up? She waited downstairs, and when Davy returned, she asked, "Want a drink?"

He did. He made himself one, and looked inquiringly at her, but she shook her head. He said, after a moment, "We'll skip the small talk. I didn't phone you while you were at Amy's. I thought you'd rather I didn't, and if you'd had anything to say I figured you'd call me. I assume you . . . told Amy?"

"Yes." She was standing quietly by the mantel. "It was like being in the bottom of a well."

"I know."

After a minute, she astonished him by saying, "I'm sorry I told her."

He was almost too amazed to speak and then he said, "It's all right with me, Meg. I didn't like the idea. I don't now, but I understand. You've always told her everything."

"Not always . . . when I was little, of course, and through the first year we were married . . . I mean about arguments or silly misunderstandings, that sort of thing" — she looked into her mind for words — "all the things that weave into a marriage. I stopped pretty soon; it wasn't loyal; whatever we did or said or thought was just between us. So, I'm sorry, now."

"Maybe she is, too," Davy said oddly, and she looked at him quickly, wondering if at any time he had heard rumors about Edwin. But his face was quiet and closed against her like a fist; not threatening; just closed as a hand might be, lying idly on a desk.

He asked abruptly, "Are you waiting for me to ask you what she said?"

"I think perhaps you know pretty much what she said."

"I was never her boy," Davy remarked without resentment, "though she likes me well enough. Perhaps she thinks this justifies the doubts she had when we were married."

"She didn't have any doubts."

"I think so. We had a few private conversations — conferences, you might call them — Amy and I," Davy told her.

"I didn't know that."

"No point in your knowing. . . . Well, what exactly did she advise?"

"She didn't, not in the way you mean."

"Now I've heard everything," Davy exclaimed.

"You're angry," she said, and her voice was uneven. "Please don't be angry, Davy. Don't let's quarrel."

He wasn't angry, not at Amy or anyone. He was frightened. He hadn't known how to deal with this before; he knew even less now. And he said, low, "I'm not angry, darling."

Her face quivered slightly as if he had struck her a very small blow and then she said, in a low, tight voice, "I have had to make up my own mind, Davy."

He said, starting to stammer, "To — to leave me? You wouldn't leave me, Meg, you wouldn't. . . ."

"No." Suddenly her face was transformed;

110

it was radiant, as if a burden had dropped from her, and she said, "I do forgive you, Davy."

He pushed back his chair, his drink tipped over, the whisky spilled, and the glass was shattered, but neither noticed. He crossed the space between them to take her in his arms and if, in that first infinitesimal second she drew away — no, not so much drew away as tightened against him the muscles of her mind and body — he did not realize it.

After a while, as they went upstairs together, he held her hand and she leaned against his shoulder.

CHAPTER 7

The reconciliation was, Davy believed, with profound gratitude, complete; yet he felt that Meg had altered. He discussed it with himself; he asked: Why not? Anything which is important to you — which precipitates suffering, causes struggle, and brings you to a decision — is bound to alter you. You mature a little.

He asked himself why, except for the painful memories of failure, of shame and humiliation and fear — he still had occasional pinpricks of fear — he himself had not changed. At least he thought he had not, but he knew that to evaluate oneself accurately is almost impossible.

As far as the change in Meg was concerned, he felt it most strongly in their sexual relationship. Meg was a responsive lover; only in the first months of their marriage had she been timid. But never had she been, in love, aggressive. Now there were times when she was. He could not define it with clarity except that her attitude was more a seizing than a sharing. The first time this occurred, he was astonished and experienced a delightful excitement. But after a while, he wondered.

Meg could not have told him why she reacted as she did, had he been able to bring himself to ask her. She knew only that she felt driven to assert a possession which, in its physical expression, appeared to bring her, briefly, some reassurance.

He tried to talk to her a few times, in order to clear up any lingering doubts, to remove any barbs which remained in her mind. But she said, "It's over; it's forgotten; we'll never speak of it again."

He told himself: She means it. Yet he did not wholly believe it. There were times when he found her looking at him with eyes which seemed to have recently ceased to cry, although he didn't think she had. And other moments, when they were out somewhere, and there were strange women present, when he saw her glance from one to another with open speculation; and still others when, talking to another woman, he'd look up to find Meg watching him, her face composed, but not her eyes.

Before they left on vacation, he had to take a trip which would keep him away overnight. He'd expected Meg to go with him but she said definitely: No, she'd rather not. It was so hot; and there was a great deal to attend to before they closed the house for their holiday. Davy had three weeks, Bob would take three. Helen, the children, and Meg would remain in Vermont until after Labor Day, and the men, during the extra time, would drive up weekends.

"But I counted on you," Davy told her, "and it's not a bad trip."

"It's so hot," she repeated. "Honestly, dear, I'd rather stay home."

He reminded her that motels were air-conditioned, but she shook her head and turned away. She said evenly, "You'll only be away a night."

When she kissed him good-by, he realized with infinite shock that she was shouting at him silently. "I trust you," her vibrant silence said. "I trust you." And he went to get into his car, wondering if, during the rest of their lives together, she would trust him with such emphasis, such deliberate, if unspoken, vigor.

It would be like a manacle. He told himself — driving along steaming highways and dusty back roads, absently noting the need for rain — that trust doesn't contemplate the need for trust; it is simply there. He hoped she would outgrow this phase of their altered relationship?

He was tired. He'd been working hard to clear his desk for the coming holiday. Possibly this was all in his mind, his imagination. He thought soberly: I still feel guilty as hell. I suppose I always shall. I read things in the book which aren't there, and magnify trifles.

It was Meg's nature to magnify trifles; now, he'd become infected.

When he returned, she was glad to see him. She asked about the trip and pressed him for details. He gave them, and saw that her eyes, as she smiled, were searching and, perhaps, anxious.

In due time they drove to Vermont in what Bob described as a multitude of cars; he and Davy took theirs. The women, Corky, and the children went in Meg's station wagon.

It wasn't a long journey and, even in the rain — for it was finally raining — a pleasant one. They stopped along the way for lunch and to let Corky run. The children were beside themselves with anticipation; Corky, too. The Watson youngsters, Cora, Peter, and Laurie, were as noisy as all children their age and very engaging. Laurie, inclined to motion sickness, had had a preventive pill at the start of the trip, and had fallen asleep. "Thank heaven," said her mother.

The cottage they leased was one of several set apart, off a good back road, and on a wide, tree-trimmed lake, very cold, and on fair days, darkly blue. They had their own small dock; there was a raft common to all the settlement, and a couple of boats came with their cottage — a canoe and a flat-bottom rowboat. The little boathouse contained fishing tackle, paddles, and oars; the simple cottage had ample sleeping and living space, a good kitchen, and a big screened front porch on which they usually ate.

Their neighbors were people who'd been coming to the Lake as long, or longer, than they had. Everyone knew everyone else. There were a number of children, and each holiday, picnics, bathing, fishing. Occasionally there'd be an informal get-together, on one or another porch, for the shore folk, and often beach picnics to which everyone contributed work and food. There was a traditional beach party, complete with bonfire, whenever there was a full moon.

The owners of the cottages had cleaned and polished after the last occupants and, according to custom, stocked the refrigerator and put staples in the cupboards. Shopping in the village, which wasn't far away, presented no problem.

No one rented for less than two weeks, most people for longer; one couple came for all summer, and many of the cottagers had occasional guests.

One day, the cottagers next door, the Hendricksons, decided to go fishing and, as they had guests, Davy offered a rowboat for any overflow. Bob had been called back to town, much to his annoyance. "I don't see why my clients can't stay out of jail on my vacation," he'd remarked, with some exaggeration. "A man needs a rest once in a while. At least this one does."

Davy was alone in camp when the Hendricksons started toward their dock. Meg and Helen had gone to the village, and the children were gathered in their usual vocal clumps along the shore.

One of the Hendricksons' guests was a business associate of his host; another a distant, much younger, cousin, a schoolteacher; there was also an elderly couple. Davy went along, and Mrs. Hendrickson, the single man, and the cousin were in his boat. The fishing wasn't much good, but the day was superb and the surroundings lovely. Davy talked to the girl, who needed some instruction in this fine art. He hadn't, during the introduction, heard her surname, but her given name was Lois. She was attractive; about twenty-five, he thought, maybe older. They talked of the school in which she taught, of the Lake, and of what was going on in the world. "Up here," Davy told her,

"I never see an urban paper; there's no television and I rarely listen to radio. When I do, it's to the nearest station, and for weather."

They agreed life was much more peaceful and uncomplicated when, briefly, you lived in ignorance. "Not that it can ever last long," said Lois.

When they all came in, having determined to by shouting across the quiet water between the boats, Davy helped Mrs. Hendrickson and Lois out, and the male guest — his name was Green — gave him a hand with the boat. Hendrickson had already beached his.

Walking up the bank, Lois tripped over a small stump and fell, twisting her ankle, exclaiming with pain. Hendrickson and Davy reached her first and helped her to her feet, but she could not stand.

Hendrickson was a middle-aged man, heavy, and with a cardiac history, so Davy picked the girl up. She was small, light — and protesting. His cottage was nearer than the Hendricksons', he said. They'd get her shoe off, and then he'd put her in the car and take her the short distance between the houses.

Meg and Helen were back on the porch when the small procession arrived. The girl was still protesting, but also laughing at something Davy was saying.

It was Helen who cried, "What happened?"

"It's not serious," Lois said apologetically, "but I've sprained my ankle, I'm afraid. It was clumsy of me. . . . I can't put any weight on it. . . . Mr. Jones is very kind," she added.

Meg said, "Put her in the lounge chair." She was experienced in first aid, as was Helen. Between them and Mrs. Hendrickson, appearing with the other guests and coaching from a perturbed side line, they got the shoe off. Meg looked at the ankle a moment, as if she expected it to be as slender as its mate; but it really was swollen.

Eventually, attended by considerable confusion, Lois was taken back to the Hendricksons'. There was a good doctor in the village, and as all the cottages had telephones, they called him to look after her.

At supper Helen said, "Poor kid . . . and she was going home tomorrow."

"I doubt she'll make it," Davy said.

"Oh, she drove up with the older couple; they'll manage," Helen said. "But what a way to end a vacation. How long was she here? . . . Cora, if you don't like what you're eating, for mercy's sake don't dramatize it by making gruesome faces. . . . And where do you think *you're* going?" she asked her son.

He told her explicitly, and was excused.

Then she laughed. "I was never more amazed in my life," she said, "than when Davy came into view bearing a maiden. I wondered if she'd been suddenly taken drunk; then I remembered not only the time of day and the fishing expedition, but the fact that last night, when we went over for cocktails, Lois drank unsullied tomato juice. But Davy, you did look so tall, dark, handsome, and Sir Lancelotish. Didn't you think so, Meg?"

"I don't know that I thought anything," Meg said, "except that the girl had been hurt."

Davy smiled at her and then looked away. He had seen her eyes. They were dark with some emotion which he believed he could identify as fear.

That night she silently forgave him again; at least, that is how he explained to himself the clinging, almost frantic closeness and the gripping, slender arms.

Whereas, at first he had been pleased at the new communicated excitement, he'd come to feel only sorrow and, as now, impatience.

"You love me, Davy? You do love me?"

"I love you, darling," he said.

"Never stop," she implored him, "never stop." And, later, she said, not knowing that she said it, "I try so hard to please you."

His impatience left him. He said, "You always please me, Meg."

At breakfast, she said, "We must walk over and see how Lois is."

So they went, the three of them, and found Lois comparatively comfortable, her departure postponed for a couple of days. Mr. Green was leaving in the afternoon and as they sat on the Hendricksons' porch, Lois complained, "Such a to-do about nothing. I'm so sorry I'm holding the Riches up."

Mr. Rich said, "Don't be, we're glad of an excuse to take a longer vacation. My business runs better without me than with me."

His wife said, "Anyway, he's practicing for retirement."

Lois turned to Davy and remarked that she was still embarrassed. "Think nothing of it," he said. "I'm always carrying beautiful young women hither and yon."

"Doesn't Mrs. Jones object?" Lois asked, laughing.

"Not really," Davy answered. "She just takes the whip down from the wall —"

Meg said lightly, "Don't listen to him. The

only catch is that I must keep my weight down so that, when he's not too busy, he can carry me."

Davy had spoken as, nominally, he would speak. Now he thought: If I have to weigh every word . . . and suddenly words became a burden and a danger. He said, "I had no difficulty carrying you over that first threshold, Meg, and you haven't gained an ounce since then."

I wonder, he thought, if I can carry her over this one? It's high. What's the room beyond it like? One that narrows into a sort of cell, or the big airy room which marriage builds? One with space for the necessary individual privacy, which in no way blocks off love, and which, therefore, needs no dividers?

Returning to the cottage, with Corky bouncing ahead of them, Meg commented, "Now that's what I consider a very attractive girl."

"She's not exactly pretty," Helen said, "but she has lots of personality. Like Cora," she added.

"What's your opinion?" Meg asked her husband.

"Very pleasant," he answered. He took Meg's hand and put it on his arm. " 'Lean on me, Grandma,' " he advised. " 'I'm almost seven,' " and Helen cried, "You should be on Quiz programs. Whenever did you read *Little Lord Fauntleroy?*"

"In another incarnation," Davy told her, "so my quote may be inaccurate. And when did you read it, Old Timer?"

"Recently," said she. "Aloud . . . to Laurie."

"I'm glad I wasn't of that generation," Davy said. "My mother was all for the correct thing, so I'd have been in velvet, with long golden curls."

"Not without cosmetic aid," Helen said. "I bet you were born with a mop of jet-black hair."

"Always regretted it wasn't with a caul," Davy said.

They were almost at the house. Meg took her hand from Davy's arm. "No tree stumps for me," she said firmly. "I look where I'm going."

From now on, she thought, I'll look, I'll watch every step. She glanced at Davy and away again, a cool, measuring glance, and, sick at heart, he thought: There are times when she hates me.

When Bob returned, he reported there had been no new scandals, only a couple of old ones, warmed over; it was hot as hell at home; the summer colds had set in and most of the avid gardeners had poison ivy. "So what's new here?" he demanded.

Helen briefed him: The Hendricksons' guest had sprained her ankle; Peter had had an infected mosquito bite, now better; and Cora had caught a good-sized perch.

The following week Amy and Edwin came up to stay at the Lodge at the end of the lake. When Amy telephoned, she said, "The kids are away on their own pressing business, and Edwin can take a few days off. . . . No, of course we don't want you to put us up. There's barely enough room at the cottage for you and the Watsons. We'll see you every day, and I'm booking you in advance for dinner at the Lodge."

The Masons arrived early in the evening, settled in, and came over next morning — with suntan lotion, insect repellent, and bathing suits — to spend the day swimming, picnic-lunching, beach-sitting, and walking. During lunch, Helen told the story of Davy's chivalry, with gestures. "His strength was as the strength of ten," she announced, "because his heart is pure."

"I could have achieved it," said Edwin modestly, "my heart's pure; but my middle thickens as my hair thins. What did the damsel in distress weigh, Davy?"

"According to my calculations, and I'm

rarely wrong," said Davy gravely, "about one hundred and seven."

"I am strong," said Bob, "but not because my heart is pure." He added dreamily, "Her measurements are approximately thirty-six, twenty-five, thirty-four."

"But you never saw — oh, I forgot, she came before you left," said Helen. "How did you come by that information?"

"Guess work, intuition, natural genius. Before I met you, love, I got around."

"I just bet you did," said Helen and beamed upon him.

"Personally," Edwin remarked, lying back in a beach chair, "I would hesitate to disclose such *expertise* to my wife. But you're a lawyer, Bob, and should know what is, or is not, circumstantial evidence."

Meg looked swiftly at her sister, but Amy was regarding the lake, her face as quiet as the cloudless sky.

Could I have been mistaken? Meg thought. Perhaps Edwin never. . . . Now she was off on a personal merry-go-round, which offered only dizziness, confusion, and no brass ring.

That night the Watson brood went whooping off to a beach party and their parents, Davy, and Meg, exchanged camp clothes for suitable attire and went to dine on excellent food and wines, with accompanying elegance and music, at the Lodge.

After dinner they danced on the great porch, overlooking the water, and Davy dutifully partnered Amy.

"You're looking well," she commented. "Thin — but then you always were. Meg's too thin, of course."

"She eats like a horse," said Davy, and quickly switched to inquiries about the Mason children. At this juncture there was little to say to Meg's sister. Dancing with her, he felt, as embarrassed as if he were naked, yet there was nothing in her conversation to indicate that she'd ever heard of a motel outside a small, strange town until, as he was taking her back to the table she said, low, "Be kind to Meg, Davy."

It was not a petition, but a warning. She would be watching; she would, if necessary? do more than warn.

Davy found dancing with Helen Watson relaxing; not only did she dance well — for that matter, Amy did, too — but she was gay, and ignorant of undercurrents and rip tides.

"We have such fun," Helen said contentedly. "I think we're the two nicest couples I've ever known. Year after year we expose ourselves to weeks of unsolitary confinement, and never get into each other's hair."

Davy agreed.

Helen was not insensitive or unperceptive, but she accepted surfaces. Now she asked, "Is Meg well, Davy?"

"As far as I know," he answered and was forced to add, "What makes you ask that?"

"I don't know . . . she isn't . . . oh, she looks fine, but somehow she doesn't seem quite herself. Is it you, Davy?" she asked.

He felt his heart plummet. Oh, no, he thought. Isn't it enough to know that Amy knows . . . but, not Helen.

Then he thought: Meg wouldn't . . . she isn't like that. Yet, how did he know what she was like now, or what she was becoming? He had, these past weeks, felt something which he could identify only as a sense of exile.

"Me?" he asked, and cleared his throat.

Helen said seriously, "I thought maybe you were having an ulcer or diverticulitis or something fashionable. Remember that night at our house when you were jack-knifing around and Meg went into a spin? That's about the only thing that would upset her. Me, I'm upset half a dozen times a week. If it isn't Bob, it's one of the kids. But Meg has only you."

Yes, that's it, or partly so, he thought with

dreadful unhappiness. She has only me.

He said, "You're a doll, Helen. And I'm fine. I had the works at Mike's not long ago and, apart from the prevalent tension under which we all appear to labor, I could join the Marines — again."

She said gravely, "I'm so glad."

He approached forbidden territory with Meg that night, which cost him something. When they had gone to bed, he said, after a false start or two, "Helen's worried about you."

"Why on earth should she be?"

He answered, "She thinks you're troubled about something."

"Well, I'm not," Meg said instantly, "unless it's what's happened to the winter curtains. Mrs. Lowry sent me a card . . . she can't find them, and the cleaner swears we didn't send them."

She thought: And suppose I'd answered, "I'll be troubled the rest of my life?"

She was disturbed to think that she had altered outwardly. And after a moment, Davy remarked dryly, "Forget it. . . . Perhaps my slip shows — on you."

Meg sat up in bed. Here they shared a bed, not a very good one. The pale, silvered light filtered in through the pines and they could hear the lake singing itself to sleep.

"I'm glad you think it's so amusing," she said.

"I didn't . . . I don't . . . It seems the simplest way to diagnose her quite genuine anxiety about you."

They were close to quarrelling and then she put her arms about him. "I'm sorry, Davy," she said humbly. "I'll try. . . ."

Try what? To do as she said she'd been doing . . . the old cliché: forgive and forget? Or to try not to show that she had not?

CHAPTER 8

The day before the Masons went home, Amy and Edwin came over for fishing and lunch. Helen and Meg went shopping and came back to await the return of the fishermen. They came in, announcing that the fish were biting great guns, and projected another expedition. Amy said she'd had enough sun, but Helen asked, "What about Meg and me?"

Amy looked thoughtful. She asked, "Would you pass up the opportunity, Meg, and go antiquing with me?"

It was an excuse to talk privately with her sister. She thought: If we stay here, even though the others are out, there'll be cottagers dropping in.

"I thought you had enough antiques to furnish a room at the Metropolitan," Davy said, and Edwin eating his way through a sandwich, said resignedly, "She has. We expect to build a wing on the house any moment."

Amy remarked that her heart was set on a small Sheraton desk; she couldn't live without it, and she had just the place to put it. "But prices in town are out of all reason," she said. "Maybe I'll have better luck here."

"Don't be too sure," Davy advised her. "The day's past when you could run up into New England or Pennsylvania and pick up treasures for the proverbial song. The dealers now know their antique onions."

Amy agreed that one rarely found bargains, but thought possibly there was something stashed away in a barn off the tourist's beaten track.

"The beaten tourist is more like it," Bob remarked. "Take your checkbook and a letter of credit."

Meg said that she'd found bargains, though not of the caliber for which Amy was looking, but she'd be glad to go along, and so it was arranged.

Meg was uneasy. She was still excoriating herself for having told Amy the wildly implausible story which was — as so many such stories are — true.

Amy didn't find her desk and, after a diligent search, she gave up; she did discover a Staffordshire pitcher and she bought Meg a luster mug, after which they drove for tea to a place not far from the Lake and overlooking a smaller body of water. Sitting in basket chairs, they were served in a garden, bright with annuals. It could have been pleasant and restful. Few people were there and most of them were inside, where it was cooler.

Amy did not bother with preliminaries. She could, of course, have talked to Meg in the car, but you keep your eyes on the road, driving. Now she said, "Meg, you're making a dreadful mistake."

"Am I?"

"You'd rather I didn't go on?"

"Yes."

"I'm sorry, but I'm going to." Amy watched the sun flash from the big diamond on her left hand. "You're creating an unfortunate impression, dear."

"On whom?"

"This isn't like you," Amy said. "So short and sharp. You're getting so you talk in as few words as possible and you're making it quite obvious that there's something wrong between you and Davy."

"There's nothing wrong between us," Meg said quietly and then locked her pretty red mouth, trying for an expression of serene indifference.

"I could shake you," Amy said, exasperated. "You can deny it as much as you want, but I'm certain your attitude is noticeable to everyone. It is to me."

"That's only because I was foolish enough to confide in you," Meg said.

132

Amy was not easily hurt, but she was hurt now. She put down her cup, crying, "But you've always confided in me!"

"Not really," Meg said. "Not after I'd been married awhile."

"Even Edwin asked 'What's the matter with Meg?' and you know," Amy went on, "except where business or politics are concerned, he's not very observant."

"I'm sorry," Meg said vaguely.

All the worn similes rose to Amy's lips — mountains out of molehills, tempests in teapots — but she said merely, "Your worst mistake is having taken this — episode — so seriously that you've permitted it to alter you."

Meg was silent and Amy added with a certain amount of desperation, "Is it possible that you don't realize this is the surest way to drive Davy into a real affair? What happened last spring wasn't real."

She thought: Providing he told the truth. But she did not say it.

Meg's expression changed; it was no longer a mask; she had now the white look of shock. She said, almost harshly, "That's absurd!"

"Not at all. If you send Davy to Coventry, he'll find a way out. There's no man easier to conquer than one who continually feels guilty and is constantly reminded of it —"

"I don't remind him."

"Perhaps not. As a matter of fact, he needn't feel guilty; all he has to feel is neglected. What follows is tea and sympathy."

Meg thought; It was Edwin after all; he'd felt neglected among Amy's multiple activities.

She said again, "I don't remind Davy, and he's not neglected." She looked at her watch, a tenth-wedding anniversary present. She very often turned it over to read the inscription on the back, but hadn't for some months. She knew what was inscribed there by heart — and wished she did not.

"We'd better go now," she suggested. "I told Helen I'd start supper, even if they don't bring home the bacon — in this case more fish. But there's enough for us all after your expedition this morning. . . . we expect you to stay, you know."

So they went back to the cottage; the fishermen returned; the children ate on the porch, the adults in a corner of the living room at a big table. Everyone was relaxed and gay. Edwin had caught most of the fish. "As usual," he said complacently, and Davy remarked that there was something about Edwin no poor fish could resist.

So the lazy days went drifting by and Davy

thought: It's no good, this waiting for each day to end, not because night will come and you can be alone with the person you love best, but because there'll be another twenty-four hours dropped into eternity, the ultimate point of no return.

When the three weeks were over, the men went back to work, the women and children remained. They'd do what they always had done: fish, swim, see the neighbors, ride herd on the children, search for the elusive antique, and look to the weekend for excitement. After the second weekend, they'd all go home.

"There's something missing this year," Helen commented one day, when she and Meg were sitting on a fallen log near the water where the children were splashing and shouting.

"I thought it was about perfect," said Meg. "We've really been very lucky in the weather."

"The weather, yes. We've been up here in some pretty discouraging weather other years, haven't we? No . . . I can't put a finger on it. Maybe it's that I feel you and Davy aren't having as much fun as usual," Helen told her friend.

"Oh, but we are," Meg protested.

"Bob's sort of distracted at times," Helen

went on, pursuing her own thoughts. "I hope he doesn't work too hard this week; he doesn't look well. When I nag him, he laughs. . . . Maybe we've outgrown the Lake," she said thoughtfully. "I know we discussed that last year after we came home. Coming here is a sort of habit, I suppose. But the kids are still crazy about it, and they scream with horror if we suggest a change — the sea, the mountains. It's been some time since we skipped a summer here — not since the year you went to Maine and we visited Bob's people in California."

Meg said, "Davy and I loved Maine. It was a different sort of vacation, although it was shorter. Davy was called back because of an impending strike, remember? Yet we often said we hadn't liked breaking the pattern, actually. . . . What in the world is Corky doing?"

"Fishing, I think," said Helen. "He seems to be standing on his head." She paused and then went on, "Perhaps we all rely too much on comfortable, accustomed patterns. If it weren't for the kids, Bob and I would try something new — an island in the sun, maybe — and make you come along. You and Davy can go anywhere you want. Europe . . . the world. You've no one but Corky to look after."

"Davy has a horror of leaving him at the vet's unless he's ill. . . . Hi, Corky," said Meg, "what were you doing?"

The dog had bounded out of the water and was tearing around the log, showering them as he passed; he smelled of fish and was tastefully draped with some kind of trailing water grass.

"Lie down, dope," said Meg. She linked her hands about her knees and looked at Helen. "I don't especially want to go anywhere," she said, "and Davy can manage only three weeks. He should have a month and will eventually, I suppose. But I can't imagine anything more tiresome than tearing around Europe in planes in just three weeks."

"Oh, well," Helen said lazily, "when the kids are in college or digging ditches —"

"Laurie and Cora?"

"They're a lot more the ditchdigger type than Peter — anyway, when they are doing whatever it is they'll do when they graduate — if they graduate —"

"According to Bob, spaceships, electronics, President of the United States."

"Somehow I can't picture Peter as President," said his mother, "though Laurie in a spaceship seems reasonable, and maybe Cora would take to engineering; she engineers now, like crazy — her life, her friends' lives, ours. Anyway, we can leave them, the four of us — you and Davy, Bob and I — will have time, and, heaven grant, money enough to take a cruise, provided we aren't falling apart from old age."

"We'll all work toward it," said Meg, "not the old age, but the time and money."

As the previous weekend, Bob drove Davy up for the last one, which extended through Labor Day. He immediately inquired of his wife and children, "Did you miss the bread-winner?" and they replied "Yes," in various satisfactory ways.

Davy asked Meg gravely, "And you — were you wretched without me?"

"At times," she answered and smiled at him, but only with her mouth.

Yet it was true enough. She had been wretched without him, but that she'd missed him, in the way Helen missed her husband, was not true. Perhaps, she thought, he felt a little as she did — profound loss, yet a relief equally deep — no sense of strain, no watching one's words or steps. She thought: But it isn't my fault. I didn't build this barrier.

They went back home, tanned, and as they assured one another, relaxed. The Mason children were miserable at having to leave, and declaimed it all the way home. They had to return to school and their mother reminded them patiently, as she did every year, that they were luckier than a lot of kids who had had to go home earlier.

Corky moped. His ears drooped and so did his tail. He was fond of the Lake where he could find such lovely dead fish. Delicious! And he was devoted to the youngsters.

Helen and Meg plunged into the seasonal madness known as "opening the house," which is very like the lunacy called "closing the house." Mrs. Lowry condescended to give Meg extra days; the curtains were found; and the telephone rang incessantly: committees, choir practice, projects . . . the familiar routine, the cushioned rut. Davy was up to his nice, flat ears in work, and this might have been any previous year, at this time — except that it wasn't.

The Hendricksons, passing through on a business trip, stopped at the Watsons for the night, and Meg and Davy went over after dinner. This also happened every autumn. During the course of the evening, Helen asked, "Do you ever hear from the Riches?"

"Yes, they're fine."

"What about — what was her name — Lois?"

"Oh, she writes; still apologetic about her accident."

"Does she ever come to New York?" asked Meg.

"She used to during a Christmas or an Easter vacation, but she's been busy getting engaged. I understand her financé's the ninth wonder of the world."

"Oh?" said Davy. "Well, he's getting a nice girl."

You keep the conversational ball bouncing or it sits on your host's rug and looks at you.

"Man's been married before," said Hendrickson, passing his glass for a refill. "He's divorced. Can't say I approve, and Lois is a lot younger."

"She's old enough to know her own mind," his wife commented, "and her Eliot — that's his name — has no children to complicate matters."

"That's the only reason I don't divorce Bob," said Helen. "Well, not really; he's also the only lawyer I know well and I couldn't ask him to take my case. But when it comes to kids, it would be so hard to divide three."

"I can always learn to saw Laurie in half," Bob suggested. "That's an act I've always fancied. . . . And when are you coming to me for your divorce, dear?" he asked Meg.

Only Davy noticed the slight quiver of her

eyelids. She answered carefully, "Almost any Tuesday, now."

"I'm busy Tuesdays," said Bob. "On Tuesdays I take my ravishing secretary to lunch, the movies, dinner, and a night club. . . . I'm sorry, Helen, but I had to explain. Meg's an old friend."

Davy laughed. Bob's secretary was a tall, narrow, hideously efficient woman with as much sex appeal as . . . He tried to think of something that had no sex appeal and came up with cold rice pudding. Maybe he was wrong. Many people liked cold rice pudding, however he might feel about it.

"Don't laugh," said Helen sadly, "you've no idea to what lengths Bob goes to keep me from knowing what I've known for years. Roses, emeralds, mink stoles, and of course, 'Sorry, darling, but I'll be up all night with a sick client.' I'm resigned, however. Someday he'll tire of this mad affair and come home for good. I've been knitting slippers for him, year after year. There are six and a half pairs in the shoe closet. When the time comes, I'll warm all of them by the fire — if it's winter — mull a little wine, and welcome his return."

"What will you do if it ends in summer?" Davy inquired.

"I've made him the sweetest hair shirt you

ever saw," Helen answered, "air-conditioned, with an embroidered *aloha* lei at the neckline."

This was the way they always talked, the Watsons and the Joneses. Not that Meg entered into it much. She provided the appreciative audience. She was not, she once told Davy, quick enough, nor given to flights of fancy.

But now she could and did join in, as if her wits had been sharpened, like a pencil, with a good knife.

Hendrickson said, "You're all crazy."

Meg spoke to Bob, "Only a Tuesday would be convenient for me."

"And I was going to advise you for nothing," Bob said indignantly, "just to act even with your husband for his superior golf. However, I can suggest something which will cost him plenty."

"What's that?" Mrs. Hendrickson asked.

"I know an excellent psychiatrist. First, I'll send Meg to him; then Davy; and after that, Corky. He'll split his fees, of course."

"Corky's another reason," said Meg, "now I come to think of it, I don't want him sawed in half."

"Of course. Custody of the canine; it's becoming as much of a problem as who gets the kids and for how long," Bob said.

Mr. Hendrickson's attention had wandered, but he now remarked that he still didn't approve of Lois marrying a divorced man, no matter how much money he had.

"Money?" Bob repeated. "What's that? Whatever it is, you mean, he has it?"

"Tons," said Mrs. Hendrickson. "She's handed in her resignation. No more school-teaching."

"If only they lived in this state . . ." Bob said mournfully. "I can draw up the best, most unbreakable, pre-marital contract you ever laid eyes on, for a nominal fee, of course."

"There's a new woman in town," Helen said presently. "Well, not exactly new. She used to visit the Warings. I can't wait till our men see her, after which I'll invite all of you and every other woman I know in town to a scratching-out-of-eyes, back-biting party."

"Ha!" said Bob. "One of the Gabors? I hope."

"No," Helen told him. "I met her yesterday. At the Club. . . . I told you, dear."

"I know, but I love it when you repeat yourself."

"The Warings are throwing a party for her next week," Helen said. "Everyone will be there and we girls will retire to the powder

143

room and cry in the powder."

"Better keep your powder dry," Davy advised.

"Who is she?" Meg asked.

"Rhoda something. Anyway, she's bought the old Crosswell place."

"That's been on the market these past hundred years."

"Three, Bob dear. Does time pass that slowly? Anyway, they've come down in price."

"Where's she from?" Davy asked.

"Montana, Colorado — somewhere out West."

Bob asked hopefully, "Was she on the stage once, or in the movies? How many times has she been married? Does scandal pursue her? Was she ever involved in a murder?"

"You read too many lurid paperbacks," his wife said indulgently and Davy flinched a little.

"I just thought a little business might come my way," Bob explained.

Helen looked pleased. She said, "I doubt if she'll need a lawyer. She is one."

"Oh, my sacred Blackstone," Bob said, jarred. "As if there weren't far too many of us in this town now!"

"She isn't going to practice. She practiced

144

with her husband, and he died a year or so ago. She came here because she liked what she saw of the town when she visited the Warings — she and Jenny were in college together somewhere — and, anyway, she wants to live in the East."

"How old is she?" Meg asked.

"Fortyish, I suppose," Helen said. "Looks about thirty."

"Just how long were you at the Club?" Bob inquired.

"Oh, about twenty minutes — just long enough to deliver a message. I had to take Cora to dancing class. . . . Want to know more?"

Mrs. Hendrickson said, "Of course."

"One son; he's just entered Yale. Another reason she wants to live in New England. Loads of money, I believe. Actually," said Helen, "you'll all like her. I do and, as a rule, I simply can't stand a beautiful woman, with the exception of Meg, of course. And you, Kate," she added to Mrs. Hendrickson.

Sometime later, the Joneses went home and Meg reflected aloud as they went upstairs, "I wonder what she's like, really?"

"Who?" asked Davy, yawning. . . . "Hey, don't trip me," he admonished Corky. "We realize you're glad we're home."

"The woman who bought the Crosswell

place. They kept that pretty much under wraps, didn't they? I didn't see a word in the paper."

"You'll soon find out what she's like," he chuckled as they reached the landing. "I can just see Bob talking shop — or is it bench? — with a pretty woman."

"I suppose the Warings will ask us to the party," said Meg, so drearily that he thought: I hope to God they don't.

They did, and the Joneses went; everyone who was asked went. Mrs. Howard — Rhoda to the Warings — was staying at the Inn while the Crosswell house was being redecorated. The closing had gone through and the lawyers for the Crosswell estate were only too glad to get it off their hands.

Meg decided that Mrs. Howard was authentically beautiful: her regular features; her astonishingly blue eyes; her dark, classically arranged hair; her enviable figure. She was also friendly.

"Must have wowed 'em in court," Bob commented during the party. "That is, if she ever was in court."

Davy liked Mrs. Howard's voice; it was low and warm. He said, "She'll be quite an addition to our hamlet."

"Helen had me worried," Bob said, "but in a pleasant, anticipatory way. I thought

146

something special in the way of man-eaters had descended upon us. I'm so susceptible; also, disappointed," he grieved.

"Oh, sure!"

"But it's true," Bob said. "It's just my good fortune that, however enticing the girls are, I always compare them with Helen. She's kept me in line since we were married. Blows the whistle on me now and then, of course, but she knows I'm harmless. Isn't that a lousy thing to know about a man? She just wants to spare me the humiliation of realizing that I don't attract any woman but herself."

Later, at home, Meg, brushing her hair, asked, "Do you think Rhoda Howard so beautiful?"

"Why, yes," said Davy. "She's quite lovely, although not type-cast the way Helen had us believing."

He came over, took the brush from her hand and pulled her back against him, looking over her head into the mirror, meeting her eyes there, and trying to smile. But he did not feel like smiling. He said, "You're the last woman in the world who needs to worry." He almost said, ". . . about other women," but caught himself in time. "Look in the mirror."

She did so and saw her own enchanting,

irregularly shaped face, the short red-gold hair tousled, a flush touching her cheekbones and brightening her blue-gray eyes, as he said to her gently, "I love you, Meg."

CHAPTER 9

The old Crosswell place consisted of a large, very old house, with good rolling acreage, woods, neglected gardens, and a spring-fed brook. Shortly after Rhoda Howard moved in, she gave a housewarming and her son, Hal, came down from the university. He was a charming, well-mannered boy, very mature and possessed of a quiet sense of humor. He was tall, like his mother but, unlike her, strikingly fair.

Meg, Davy, and the Watsons went together and, as Helen had said of the Warings' party, "Everyone was there."

People drifted about the living room, which once, years ago, had been three rooms, and on to the terrace, for the autumn wind was soft, remembering summer. Davy, talking to a group of friends, observed Rhoda; she seemed so serene a person that his heart warmed to her. She moved among her guests, most of whom she'd met only recently, without haste, and with unforced, genuine cordiality. She was an unobtrusive hostess; you did not even know she was looking out for you, seeing that you had a chair, or a drink, or appetizers, and that you were never alone.

On the way home, Davy commented, "It was a pleasant afternoon. Everything seems to run very smoothly there. I like what Rhoda's done so far to the house. She told me it was only a beginning, and I heard her tell someone else that, whatever she may do later, she's pledged herself not to spoil it."

Meg said, "I thought it a little on the dull side. The party, I mean."

"Maybe that's because we didn't meet anyone new," Davy suggested, smiling.

"Perhaps. Of course, her house runs smoothly, rather like Amy's. Anyone can give fabulous parties with the help she has — Rhoda Howard, I mean. . . . I wonder where she found them?"

He answered, marveling at the devious ways of women, "Maida Waring told Helen that Rhoda brought the couple with her from the West; the others are local people."

"Rhoda's from Colorado," said his wife. "I was talking to the boy — he's most attractive — and it seems that his father was born in the East, but went West, very young, for his health. He graduated from college there, went to Yale Law school and then returned to Colorado to practice. She — Rhoda — is Denver born."

"You do get around," said Davy, "you and Helen."

So did he, for he already knew most of this. In a moment with Rhoda alone, on the terrace, she'd said, "I miss the mountains."

He'd asked which ones, and she'd told him; she had also spoken at some length about her husband.

Davy did not see Rhoda Howard again until one Saturday. The day was fair, still warm; the trees were starting to blaze, the sky was washed with marvelous blue and crowded with fat white clouds. He went to the golf course, looking for a game; Bob was laid up with a virus. Davy, arriving alone, saw Rhoda getting out of her car, and went to meet her.

"I didn't know you played," he said.

"After a fashion," she admitted. "I still do all the things I was brought up to do: golf, tennis, ride, swim. I like exercise and since I stopped practicing law, I have to fill up my time. You can't watch TV and read twenty-four hours a day. Fortunately I also ski and skate or what would I do when winter comes and I rattle around alone in that house, except when Hal comes home?"

He asked, "Playing with anyone?"

"No. I had an early errand in the village,

and my clubs were in the car. The Warings have put me up for the Club; meantime I've a guest card, so I came on the spur."

"Would you consider me?" he asked.

"I would," she said, "— and gratefully."

She played a good game and didn't apologize because it was no better. He thought, as they walked around the course, their caddies following: What a nice woman, so warm and tranquil.

They lunched together at the Club. Meg never expected him when he was playing and when he reached home she asked, "Find someone to play with?"

"Rhoda Howard. . . . She arrived there alone, just as I did."

"Oh!" said Meg. "What sort of a game does she play?"

Her voice was expressionless, but he looked at her skeptically, answering, "Good enough."

"You had lunch?"

"Yes . . . it's still warm enough to eat outdoors."

"How in the world did she get in?" Meg inquired. "There's a waiting list as long as your arm."

"She's not a member yet," he said, "but the Warings arranged for her to play as their guest until she is; they've put her up. Since

Waring's president and Maida's chairman of the membership committee, it shouldn't be too hard."

"I'll have to have Rhoda here for dinner some night," Meg said, "but we don't know any unattached men . . . under eighty, that is."

"I doubt it would bother her," Davy said.

"I'm sure it wouldn't," Meg agreed smoothly.

She was frightened. This was a woman whose attraction she was forced to admit: an unattached woman and, Meg assumed, brilliant. She'd always been somewhat in awe of professional women, particularly doctors and lawyers . . . not that she'd ever actually met a woman lawyer before.

The long, brilliant autumn slid almost imperceptibly into winter. Davy was working hard; he was jumpy; he went once to Mike Miller to ask irritably, "Isn't there something you can give me to keep me from flying without wings?"

There were, of course, the tranquilizers, which Mike could recommend, in moderation. He asked, after putting the blood-pressure cuff on Davy's arm, not once, but three times, "What's on your mind, Buster?"

"Work."

"Nuts! You've always thrived on work. Must be something else. I've known you — and been your doctor — ever since you moved here. Perhaps I could do more for you if I knew more. Suppose you let me guess. It's routine when the patient offers no information. . . . Financial difficulties?"

"No more than usual with a house to keep up and taxes to pay and the way they're rising. Property taxes especially. But you know all about that."

"I sure do. . . . Longevity? You're a little young to start worrying, and trying to figure how long you have left. In any case, despite the tensions, I've reassured you, time and again, in all honesty."

"I'm all right," Davy said, "except for the damned jitters."

"Oh, there's one more classic question. . . . Domestic difficulties?"

"No . . . well, in a way. Meg and I appear to have reached a sort of impasse."

"How long since?"

"Oh, last spring, perhaps," Davy said carefully.

"Any reason?"

"She thinks so. I don't. I'm sorry, Mike, I can't discuss it," Davy said wearily. "We'll have to work it out in our own way and time."

"All right," said Mike and drew his red brows together. He was puzzled. The Joneses' marriage had seemed to him, as their friend and physician, unusually good. He liked Davy somewhat better than Meg, but he thought her a pleasant and very pretty woman, although she seemed to him at times somewhat shallow. But to be fair, he did not know her well, although she was often in his office and his home.

The usual factors in domestic difficulties, he thought, didn't apply here — drinking, neglect, running around with some other woman or man.

He said, "Well, have it your own way, but if ever there's a time you feel you'd like to talk, and get it off your chest, I'm around."

"Thanks," Davy said, "but the crazy thing is there's nothing to talk about; or, very little. Forget it, Mike. Maybe I'm just tired, not work tired, but neurotic tired."

"Could be," said Mike casually.

He thought: Tired of what — of Meg, the town, the job? One of these questions he could ask, so he did, "Tired of the job, Davy?"

"No, I like it," Davy answered truthfully. "I've had other offers recently; I don't want 'em. There are times, of course, when I could kick the job out of the window, throw my resignation on a desk, and steam out. I daresay everyone feels like that once in a while. It doesn't last."

"Where'd you steam out to?" Mike inquired.

"Oh, to all the places I've never seen," Davy answered with his slow smile, "but, the impulse is soon over."

"We all reach that point, especially, after forty — which you aren't. Except to the ebullient, things are apt to stale at intervals, so, you have to make an adjustment."

Davy said, "I'll let you know how I feel after I'm forty. I haven't long to go."

He returned to the office, dictated some letters, had a conference or two, and thought: What is there to tell? Just about the — what was it? — springboard. He reminded himself: I dove into an empty pool. And after that, the guilt, the scenes, the inability to extenuate or to understand; the reconciliation, the forgiveness . . . and the departure of his wife.

For she had left him, he believed; not physically, but — he groped for a clear word. Emotionally? Spiritually? He'd sat in church recently, listening to the choir and to Dr. Carstairs preaching on spiritual love. The sermon was based on man's relationship to his God and, on the level of everyday experience, to his fellow man.

Davy had thought: But I don't know what it *is*, this spiritual love.

He knew, he thought, what it was not; it was not the urgency of the flesh, or even the compatibility of minds, or simple uncomplicated companionship. He thought, as he prepared to leave the office: Is it understanding? Is it trust?

At his house, he found Rhoda Howard having tea with his wife. When he came in, Meg jumped up and put her arms around him. She said, "Darling, I'm so glad you came home early."

He hadn't had such a welcome in months. Privately he thought: She's overdoing it. But Rhoda wouldn't know. He said, "So am I," and then, pleasurably astonished to see her, "Hi, Rhoda." They were all on given name terms, in the easy way of the community.

Rhoda said, "Meg's been trying to pressure me into working on some of her committees."

The special one, Meg explained, was a welfare project, and she added, "We could use a legal mind, particularly a woman's."

"Oh," Rhoda said, "my legal mind's getting rusty. There was a time when I thought nothing on earth could make me give up my profession. It's curious how, when the time comes, you can, and of your own volition.

157

I'm bored sometimes," she admitted. "I've been used to a very occupied life and a big city, and frankly, golf, parties, and seeing Hal now and then isn't enough. Maybe committee work would help. Just now I'm reading seed catalogs and making plans. Could be I'll go in for gardening in a big way."

Meg said, "You think the committee thing over. . . . What made you give up your practice, Rhoda?"

"Sam's death. We'd worked together ever since our marriage and when he died, the excitement went out of it; it became flat, tasteless, like something which needs salt. No one to talk things over with; no one to argue, discuss — even quarrel — with." Her dazzling blue eyes, looking directly at Meg, were nevertheless remote, and after a moment she said, "We'd expected to retire, together, when we were old — but not too old — and take a trip around the world."

Meg remarked with unusual vigor, "Perhaps he wouldn't have wanted you to retire."

"I daresay not," Rhoda agreed, "but there it is."

When she'd gone and Davy and Meg were at dinner, she said, "Just the same I think she's selfish."

"Who and why? . . . You do have a grasshopper mind, dear."

"Rhoda — and not only selfish, but a quitter. If she's as clever as Tom Waring says she is, she has no right to deprive people of her special talents. Of course," she added, "if she had to earn her living, she would have been forced to keep her practice."

He looked at her in some astonishment. It was unlike Meg to voice strong opinions. For years she'd waited for his.

He said slowly, "You're right, of course, but the heart's gone out of her."

"You have to go on just the same," Meg said, "heart or no heart."

Maybe that was a clue; maybe that was why he was living in a pleasant house under a secure roof with this shell of a woman; the heart having gone out of her, she was going on just the same. She looked as usual. She was always — no, nearly always — as familiar to him as his own face in a mirror. She was physically present, but a stranger; one who kept their house, who drove a station wagon to market, who entertained friends and was entertained in turn; who played contract, danced at the Club, cooked their meals, and slept on the bed next to his.

They took their coffee into the living room and Meg said, "If she didn't have all that money . . ."

There she was grasshoppering back to

Rhoda, although they'd spoken of a dozen things in between.

"Yes, I know; you said as much before. It's true and, perhaps, a pity."

The grapevine reported that it was a lot of money: Rhoda's from her parents, from her husband, and from her share of the practice.

Meg set down her cup and the spoon clinked on the delicate saucer. She said, "I'd forgotten. Helen and Bob are coming over. I'll put the things in the dishwasher; you sit there and read the paper. You look tired."

"Not too tired to clear," he said, and did so. Fond as he was of their friends, he wished they were not coming this evening; he felt that something had gone from their relationship. What was it Rhoda had said in another connection. Salt? Well, the easy, old comradery, the give and take, the silly jokes. . . . The Watsons hadn't changed, he thought; but he had; and, Meg.

During the evening Bob said, "I'm for bed early. I haven't felt a hundred per cent since I had that damned virus. What a lovely word, covering a multitude of ailments. No one has anything explicable, solid, and old-fashioned any more. 'You've a virus' they tell you happily and sometimes they even add, 'A new one!' "

160

Davy regarded his friend with concern. He said, "Come to think of it, you do look washed out."

"Don't be negative," said Helen briskly. "He's just trying to get sympathy. Maybe what he had wasn't a virus, but whatever it was, holy cat, what a patient! Bells ringing, fretful voice shouting . . . up and down stairs, a million times . . . What is it, dear? . . . Water . . . pills . . . one window open, another shut . . . read to me . . . go away, let me sleep. It was murder, worse than the kids."

"She loved it," said Bob. He smiled at his wife. He said, "You know you're scared stiff if I cut my little finger."

"I wouldn't be if you cut your throat," she told him, but Davy saw how anxious her eyes were.

"I'm an old, old man," said Bob solemnly. "Maybe I should ease up, get myself a partner."

"You have one," said his wife.

"I was thinking of a beautiful woman. I wonder if I could persuade Rhoda back to the Blackstone?"

"I doubt it," Helen remarked. "What's in it for her?"

"Being with me; and, also, a modest living."

"Which she doesn't need," said Meg.

"Me or the stipend?"

"Both."

"You forget," said Bob, "the priceless opportunity to associate herself with a capable, if plodding, colleague, who has, if I may say so, without immodesty, considerable charm."

Helen shrugged. She said, "She's probably been exposed to considerable charm all her life."

"Oh, well," Bob admitted, "maybe you're right. I suppose a woman around the office would cramp my style."

"In what way?" Davy inquired.

"Let's not go into that."

"You've several around your office," Helen reminded him austerely, "and they haven't cramped your style noticeably."

"Overpaid slaves," said Bob, "always forgetting their allegiance to the master, and rushing off to be married. No. I meant that with a female partner I couldn't tear off my shirt and hurl water coolers across the room, and, what's more, my language would have to be moderated."

Meg said, "I can just see you casting the first water cooler!"

They all looked at her in some surprise, and Bob said, "Any Friday, around eleven, if I'm not in court. Come to watch someday. Bring your catcher's mitt. The slaves will have locked themselves in the supply closet. I'll be happy to have you aboard, and, of course, no admission."

He soon collected his wife, they said good night, and when the car drove off, Davy remarked, "I don't like the way Bob looks."

"It probably takes a long time to get over whatever it was he had," Meg said. "Will you put the table away, Davy, please?"

It had just begun to snow, a gentle snow, falling straight; until the wind rose, later, there was no sound. "Put a coat on," Davy said, "and come out on the porch. Lord, it's beautiful."

So Meg put a coat around her and they stood together and watched the downward-drifting white. "It looks as if we were in for it. As usual they didn't forecast this one," Davy said.

He took a deep breath of the cold, still air, scented with snow — it had a scent as identifiable as any other fragrance. The trees were already powdered, and there was a spectacular, full moon.

"So long before Christmas, too," Meg complained. "When I think of the shopping and the driving and the chores ahead . . ." She shivered and he said, "You're cold; we'll go in."

He thought: Christmas. . . . This was a

town given to seasonal celebration — not merely the usual dances and parties; not only the increased church attendance, or the gifts and trees, the lights and decorations, the gaiety. There was a glowing spirit in the small community. The townspeople prided themselves on that spirit; they did not, in shops or on streets, or in their homes, permit the garish, the so-called sophisticated, the extravagant and exaggerated. On Christmas Eve there were carols on the village green, and young carolers came to the houses. Meg had always been as excited as a child about Christmas, and particularly, since they had lived here.

This year she made out her list, consulted Davy, as usual, and, as usual, started to shop early. It was all planned as it had been for a long time: one party here, another there; the Christmas Eve singing and church. The Watsons would come to them for Christmas dinner; they would go to the Watsons' New Year's Eve; the children would be put to bed upstairs and wakened at twelve to see the New Year in. At the Club there would be various holiday-week festivities and Rhoda was planning a special party for friends who were coming from Denver to visit her.

Davy thought: I wonder how I'll get through it? And how Meg will?

CHAPTER 10

Christmas, for Meg and Davy, was a pageant: snow on roads and roof and trees; candles in windows; lights exploding into color; friends and bells and wrappings of gold and scarlet, green and blue. Christmas was church, and the choir carolers, standing under clear stars, almost knee-deep in trodden white; it was a flutter of cards and wings; it was Corky going crazy with the sounds, the odors, the tissue, and tinsel. It was also, this year, a body of dark water, thickened by ice. . . . How thick? Could you skate on it? Could you glide over the uncertain surface, seeing no reflection, and reach the other side without the sudden, then the widening, crack?

On the afternoon of Christmas Eve, regarding the living room tree, Meg remarked that it was prettier than ever, and Corky barked in agreement. He was a creature for whom everything that crackled, whether paper or fireplace logs, held an obsessive attraction.

Meg had a sure, but delicate, touch with tree trimming, and with house decoration; just right; not too much of anything. She stood there, in a red dress — she always wore red at this season — and her hair was brighter than the yellow feather coiffures of the angels on the mantel.

Davy agreed and, touched an ornament with a gentle finger; it was a little gold metal bell and it swung and spoke.

All through their married life they had collected Christmas ornaments for the tree, the house, and the doors. They told each other in the early years that the children would love them. In those years the trees had been small, now they were as tall as the ceiling permitted.

Davy put an arm around his wife. The little bell had ceased to swing and chime. He said, "It's always lovely, Meg."

She turned, put her face against his shoulder and said, in a muffled voice, that she hoped he'd like what she had for him this year.

Meg planned all year, every year. She squeezed dimes and quarters from her allowance and from the small personal income left her in trust by her father, so that she could bring home, well before Christmas, a special gift for Davy.

"Don't I always like it?" he asked.

Locked away, he had for her, a mink stole; she'd wanted one for some time.

So they'd give each other gifts, but not, this year, the essential gift of themselves, each offering to the other that which cannot be bought or wrapped, the enduring gift.

Yet, it could not be enduring after all — could it? — for it had been given, year after year, yet now it had vanished. Or was it simply diminished, or merely, just out of sight and reach?

Meg drew away. She asked, "Would you run up to Rhoda's for me, dear?"

"What for?"

"I've something for her. I forgot to deliver it last time I was out."

"What on earth is it?" he asked, astonished, but knowing that Meg's gift list increased almost every year.

"Only little jams and relishes. . . . I found some pretty, small containers with colored tops, and wrapped each one separately. Mrs. Lowry and I put up a lot, remember?"

"She'll like them," said Davy. "That was sweet of you."

"Oh, the woman who has everything . . ." she began and then added, "No one has everything really. . . . How about getting going?"

They always spent Christmas Eve alone. Meg loved the Eve, the sense of anticipation

— and not for presents. They'd go, as usual, to the carols, where they'd see most of their friends, and then to a short church service. They had a custom of late tea, real tea, in the afternoon; and on return from church, a pick-up supper.

Tomorrow the five Watsons would descend upon them for an early afternoon dinner . . . this gave the Watson children leisure to scream and whoop about their own house before going visiting. For help with dinner, Mrs. Lowry had as always, her very efficient niece, Myrtle.

Davy said, "I'll go now, and walk. I'd rather, than drive."

The Crosswell — now the Howard — place was about half a mile away. It was not yet the early December dusk.

Meg went into the kitchen and returned with a big hatbox. She opened it and Davy looked into it; there were the little jams and jellies and condiments each wrapped and tied with little bows. On top of them was a wreath, of greens and holly. Meg was clever with her hands and greatly in demand at Garden Club shows, as well as when decorations were required at the high school or anywhere else. She had tied a red satin bow at the base of the wreath, and wired into place two small ceramic angels, taken from her own ornaments.

She said of the wreath, "It's small, but pretty, I think, and this is Rhoda's first Christmas in that house."

"You do like her, don't you?" Davy asked.

Meg widened her eyes. "Of course; enormously," she answered.

She did not ask, "Do you? . . . And how much?"

He took the hatbox and went trudging out in his heavy boots and clothes and walked along a quiet road on which the trees wore ermine. Few cars passed; everyone was at home, or last-minute shopping in the village, or on their way to Grandmother's, he reflected. The day was windless, clear, and very cold, and now and again snow fell from the trees with a small sound. He looked about as he walked, liking the sudden emergence of the evergreens and the bare black boughs of maples and elms. The sun was setting in a caldron of rose and gold and a faint green began to stain the sky; the green you see only in winter, along the horizon.

He had half expected Rhoda to be out, but she wasn't; she was there with Hal; they had the record player going and were laughing together in the enclosed sun porch, where the big tree stood.

Unhurried, she came into the wide entrance hall, the tall boy following. She said, "Davy, how nice! Merry Christmas," and drew him into the living room, where a fire burned upon the hearth.

This house had considerable built-in charm. Davy had always liked it; he'd known it well, if not intimately, when the last of the Crosswells he loved had lived here. Rhoda had preserved the charm and added something of her own. For all its size the house was friendly and tranquil.

"You're just in time for a drink," said Rhoda.

"I didn't come for that," he said, smiling, "and I have to get back to Christmas Eve high tea. . . . Here's an offering from Meg."

"May I open it now?" asked Rhoda.

"Yes . . . it's for now," Davy said.

She opened it, and exclaimed with pleasure. "How charming," she said. "Did Meg make everything herself?"

"Oh, yes," said Davy, "she likes creating things."

"I've just the place for the wreath," Rhoda decided. "In my bedroom . . . come up, both of you and see." Davy and Hal followed her upstairs to the big room in which there was a fireplace with holly and greens along the mantel.

"There," said Rhoda, gesturing gaily.

170

"Take the painting down, Hal . . . it can go right there."

"Murder!" said the boy. "She's had me running up and downstairs, dashing about with ladders, and whacking my thumb with hammers all day. I'm bushed."

"Hot bath, liniment, sympathy," said his mother, "but you've had a good deal of help and I don't think you're so delicate you can't manage one more wreath before you collapse. . . . Then we'll go back downstairs for that drink."

Hal officiated at the little bar and Davy — "Do take off your coat," said Rhoda — stretched out in a big chair and sighed. The house smelled of flowers — there were many of them, cut and blooming — of greens and pine and, he thought, sniffing, of cookies.

He stayed only long enough for a short drink; Hal departed after giving it to him, vanishing upstairs with hammer, nails, and wire. They could hear him banging around.

"I like your boy," Davy said.

"So do I." She added, "He's very like his father; not a carbon copy, of course — I wouldn't really like that — but in coloring and other ways."

"What was his father like?" Davy asked, without thinking. Then he said, "Sorry . . . I didn't mean to —"

"Don't be silly. I love to talk about Sam. . . . What was he like? I don't know that I can tell you, for he wasn't like anyone else — at least, so I think. He wasn't like anyone I'd known before or have known since."

He asked gently, "This is your first Christmas without him?"

"No, the second." She looked at him quietly. "I thought I couldn't manage the first. I wanted to go somewhere alone where no one had ever heard of Christmas. But there was Hal. Maybe it will get easier each time, at least in a surface sort of way." And then she added, looking through the French doors to where the tree stood, not lighted except as the lamplight shone on it, "All the years Sam and I were together, it was Christmas almost every day." She smiled. "But then you and Meg know all about that.'

He almost said, "Yes, we did once, I suppose," but instead he smiled and did not answer and Rhoda, not looking at him, thought: Is something wrong there?

Of course she knew the Joneses only slightly. Everyone said of them, "They have a wonderful marriage." And certainly they presented a picture one could admire, one that many people must envy. But when you didn't really know people — sometimes even when you thought you knew them — such pictures lacked dimension, and seemed cut out of firm, well-colored, well-shaped cardboard.

When Hal came down, Davy rose to leave; they all shook hands and spoke of the carols and of their next meeting. The Watsons had asked Rhoda and Hal to come by New Year's Eve; and during the week between Christmas and New Year's, Rhoda was giving her party. She said, at the door, as the elderly, straight-backed butler opened it, that she'd call Meg at once.

She stepped outside with Davy, a sweater tossed across her shoulders, and when he warned, "You'll take cold," she answered that she never did. And then he left, waving at her and Hal.

Returning to her bedroom to admire her son's accurate eye before she telephoned Meg, Rhoda stood for a moment at a window. She could see Davy walking down the road; in the short time he'd been in the house a wind had risen. It was at his back, and he walked with his hands in his pockets, hunched a little forward. And Rhoda said, thinking aloud, "That's a lonely man, I think."

Hal had followed her upstairs to see if the wreath were exactly placed. He'd come in just in time to hear his mother's remark, and asked, "Since when have you taken to talking to yourself, Mom?"

"Long time ago; but I haven't started answering myself yet."

"I think you're wrong. I haven't seen Mr. Jones often, but to me he's just the reverse. Mrs. J. is awfully pretty, they have loads of friends, and the little I've talked with him, he's always gay and — well — outgoing, in a quiet sort of way."

"You're right, as usual," agreed his mother. "I haven't the least idea why I said that. Maybe it's just the way he looked going down the road."

When Davy reached home Meg said, "Tea's ready."

"Fine. I'm hungry. The walk did me good. I stayed long enough to have one drink and see Hal hang the wreath. It's a great success. The jellies, too."

"Yes, Rhoda phoned. . . . Take off your things," she said. "I've set the card table in the living room."

Tea and sandwiches and little cakes; this, too, was traditional. Presently they would go out. They talked and Davy thought the house was as quiet as Rhoda's except for the little voice of their fire and their own voices, but it was not tranquil. Had it ever been? he wondered, looking back. He'd thought so, but how can you be sure?

At the carols they saw Hal and Rhoda. They were some distance away, across the green, standing near the small portable organ. Both were singing vigorously, holding their carol sheets in mittened hands. In the press of people — for many were there, even from neighboring villages — Rhoda was noteworthy. She wore a white fur coat, cut like a man's overcoat; she had a sprig of holly on a lapel; her mittens and her storm boots were red. Hal had a knitted cap over his blond hair, but Rhoda was hatless.

"Honestly," said Helen Watson, standing next to Meg, "that Rhoda's a dream; and I do like the way she enters in."

But all Meg said was, "I wonder what fur that is?"

When, after greeting numberless friends, Davy and Meg returned from the carols and church, she went to the kitchen to assemble the trays while he mixed himself a drink and concocted a mild one for her. When, later, he made himself another, she asked, "Aren't you drinking more than usual?"

"I don't think so — a short one at Rhoda's, two here. In any case I don't feel them."

Corky came up and put his head on Davy's knee; he stroked the long silky ears and then asked, as Meg left the room,

"Where are you going?"

"To bed . . . you haven't forgotten that the Watsons come tomorrow and there'll be a lot to do?"

"Myrtle will be here."

"Yes, of course. But, I'm tired."

He thought, but did not say, that they wouldn't be awakened, as the Watsons and thousands of other people would be, by children tearing into the bedroom before dawn.

After a while, he followed her and stood looking out a window in the bedroom. The northeast wind had dropped and the stars looked down upon the snow and the ice.

He was undressing when she said, "I didn't expect you'd stay at Rhoda's; I thought you'd just leave the hatbox."

This irritated him. So that was what she had been thinking about all these hours, at tea, at the carol singing, at church, and at supper. He said shortly, "I didn't stay long . . . she heard me speak to the butler at the door, so she and Hal came out; she asked me to have a drink and to see where Hal would put the wreath. What's so unusual about that?"

"Nothing." Meg wore a blue nightgown, and he saw with extreme detachment, the lines of her body, still firm and young, and slim, through the sheer material.

"You sent me there," he reminded her, in exasperation.

"I know." She sat down at the dressing table and delicately creamed her face with long strokes, and then took off the cream with tissue. "I just didn't expect you to stay so long."

"Well, I did; all of half an hour." His voice rose without his volition. "Meg, you asked me to take Rhoda a gift, from you; not me. I did. It was a cold walk; she asked me to have a drink and I did. Hal was there; he —"

She swung around on the bench. "Why are you trying to defend yourself?" she asked mildly.

"I'm not trying to defend myself!"

But she interrupted, ". . . if of course you have no reason to —"

"For heaven's sake, Meg!" He was shouting now. "I've told you . . . you asked me to go over there. I did. I stayed a half an hour."

"So you said . . . or an hour perhaps. Time flies," Meg remarked.

"If I did — but I didn't — what does it matter?"

Meg answered, fitting a net over her brushed bright hair, "It doesn't . . . except that, of course, you might have known her before."

He was shocked into stammering, "I n-never laid eyes on her until she m-moved here!"

Meg spoke in a soft, almost dreaming voice. "Rhoda told me once she'd driven, alone, all over this part of the country before she made up her mind to look for a house here."

Davy was sitting down, taking off his left shoe. He flung it violently to the floor. He said, quite aware that no man in his undershorts had dignity, "Well, what of it?"

But he knew.

Meg said, "Nothing, except she could have stopped at a motel, any motel, last spring."

"She didn't stop at any motel I was in," said Davy.

He finished undressing, went to the bathroom, returned in his pajamas and got into bed. His bed was very cold. This was Christmas Eve and his bed was cold.

He snapped off the bedside light and, a moment after, hers went out also. Tension rose in him and tightened into a knot in his neck. He moved his head from side to side upon the pillow.

He was cold and it wasn't the sheets. Of course, they'd be cold. He'd forgotten to turn on the electric blanket. He did so and the little light glowed at him like a fallen star.

Anger can make you cold; he shook with it.

After a while Meg spoke, "I'm sorry, Davy," she said.

He asked as quietly as possible, "Just what kind of a mind have you, Meg?"

"I didn't have, until . . ." She began to cry, and it had been some time since she had cried, in his presence at least. He was still, lying stretched out in the narrow bed. The thought occurred to him: It's like a rehearsal; that's what we all come to, sooner or later; a cold and narrow bed, unshared.

For the blanket did not warm him, save externally.

She said again, "I'm sorry . . . I know it didn't mean anything."

He asked stonily, "What didn't?"

"Rhoda . . . your staying . . . I do like her, Davy, but . . ." Her voice blurred and he could not hear what, if anything, she said after that.

Presently he asked, "Then every woman we've met since last spring has been — every one we meet from now on will be, suspect?"

There was no answer. Meg sobbed once or twice, quietly, drearily, and he concluded, "So, that's it."

"How do I know, Davy?" she asked

piteously. "How do I *know?*"

He answered flatly, "You don't."

A few minutes later he heard the sound of her bare feet on the hooked rug by her bed; he felt her approach, the weight and warmth and softness. She lay beside him, close, her arms about him.

She said, "I can't help it, Davy . . . only you can help me."

He put his arms about her and thought, burdened with an immense fatigue: For the rest of my life . . .

Who was the woman he had briefly met? Her name was Vivian. He had almost forgotten what she looked like except that she was small and had red hair. He thought inconsequently: Only her hairdresser knows for sure. More than this and the facts that she'd said she was forty and had a job, that she drank too much and was aware of it, he did not know.

"It's my fault," said Meg humbly. "I try not to remember."

A furious anger boiled up within him. He shook her slightly. She did not complain — it was as if, at that moment, she welcomed violence. He said, "So, all right — remember; but remember to forget."

"Please forgive me. I do trust you, Davy. I do," she said.

His grip tightened; and she cried out, feeling his fingers in her flesh. He said, "Then, for God's sake, Meg, simplify it. Stop trusting me; then we'll know where we stand."

Meg wrenched herself away and sat up in bed. She reached blindly for the switch of his bedside lamp, but her hand was shaking and the lamp crashed to the floor. She felt as if she had been struck a bruising blow. Her mind ached with it, and her heart.

"Meg?" He put out his hand, but she was no longer there. "I'm sorry," he said inadequately.

They were both sorry; they'd kept on saying it, at intervals, all this time. "I'm sorry . . . I'm sorry. . . ."

Sorry is not enough.

He heard her stumble across the little distance, her own light went on and she sat on the edge of her own bed, looking down. The first thing she said was, "My pretty lamp . . ."

Davy could see the marks of his fingers on her shoulder, and the ruins of the lamp. It was one of a pair: Meg had looked for a long time for a pair of old lamps, painted in the tones of the room. She had been like Columbus when she found them.

Now she folded her hands so they no longer shook perceptibly, and Davy got up and went to pick up the shattered lamp.

Meg said mechanically, "Be careful, you'll cut yourself," and then, "I don't suppose it can be mended."

No, it was past mending.

"I'll get a dustpan," Davy said and padded out to the utility closet in the hall, flicking on lights. He returned with the dustpan and a small long-handled broom. The broken china, which had preserved its wholeness and pattern for close to a hundred years, tinkled in fragments of white and blue and yellow, into a metal container.

She said, "Maybe I can find milk glass." She'd looked for matching milk-glass lamps, and for a long time had not found them. When she had, she'd thought they were too expensive.

He said, "Perhaps."

"You did cut yourself after all," she said.

"It's nothing."

A little cut, clean enough, a little blood.

He had detached the lamp from the outlet; now he carried it — the bulb was broken, the base almost intact — into the hall and dumped it into the metal basket which stood in the big closet. He returned for the dustpan, and its contents. When everything was disposed of, he turned off the hall and closet lights and came back into the room.

Meg apparently hadn't moved. She said, "You'd better put something on your hand."

"Get back into bed," he said, "you'll take cold — you're shivering."

She got into bed as obediently as a child or a docile hospital patient, and pulled the covers over her. Davy went into the bathroom for an antiseptic and a strip of adhesive. When he returned, she was lying there small and straight.

He closed the windows; the air was icy and, except for the bite of the wind, sweet. He put on a robe and went to sit on her bed.

"I'm sorry," he said again. How could he explain to a bruise on a shoulder, a bruise on the mind, that when your frayed nerves snapped, when the raw spot was touched, you cried out, hit out?

"It's all right," she said after a moment, "but I didn't — I don't understand you, Davy. . . . Stop trusting you?" she asked. "What does that mean? Does it mean, it's no use? That I can't trust you?"

It was like talking through a glass wall; you could see someone there, but that person heard nothing, nor when she spoke, did you. You heard only your own words bouncing back at you.

He said helplessly, "I can never make you

see — it's just that I feel you are screaming at me — yes — screaming all the time . . . in your mind . . . if I speak to a woman, if I dance with someone, if I stop at a friend's, as I did this afternoon, and stay for a little while. . . . Usually you don't say anything; this time you did."

" 'Screaming,' " she repeated and creased her brows as though this were a strange word, one she'd never heard before.

"In your mind," he said again, "trying to communicate without words and succeeding . . . as if you kept saying, 'See, I trust you'; as if I were a paroled prisoner, as if I were a thief and you looked at the cash register and said, 'I trust you' and then counted."

She said, "But it's you who can't understand. I do trust you, Davy."

"Do you?"

A clock struck and she said, in a high forlorn voice, "It's Christmas," and began to cry again.

It was a terrible effort to take her in his arms and rock her as one would a child. . . . Yes, it was Christmas.

Long after she was asleep he lay quietly in his own bed, his arms crossed behind his head. He felt no irritation now, nor anger — that had shattered as had the lamp — only a dull and heavy sorrow.

CHAPTER 11

In the morning, while Davy still slept, Meg went carefully downstairs and started break-fast. When she looked at the tree and the packages around it, she looked away again.

As was their custom, their special gifts for each other would be given at the breakfast table. Davy had propped the furrier's box against her chair the night before, after she'd gone upstairs. The jeweler's box, containing the cuff links she had bought him, was in her apron pocket. Now she put it by his plate.

They opened their packages, said the appropriate things, and kissed each other, because that, too, was custom. This is what happens in a marriage which has lasted, as they say, fourteen years; something may go wrong with the record, but the needle slides into the accustomed groove.

They had a busy morning, getting ready for their guests. But to this, also, they were accustomed. Mrs. Lowry's niece appeared in good time and capably took over. The house soon smelled delectably of turkey and dressing.

That day, like the one before, was bright and clear, and after a while the Watsons came. The children tore in, excited, already glutted with home gifts, and hungry for food. There were more presents for them under the tree, and food in abundance on the table. The children received things they really wanted, for Meg had conferred with Helen. Bob took his new putter in his hands and said to Davy, "You son of a gun. When did I give myself away?" And Helen could hardly be detached from her new pewter pitcher.

While the children examined their presents — books for Peter, a special doll for Laurie, a simple chemical set for Cora — Meg and Helen went upstairs and Helen asked almost at once, "Whatever happened to the lamp?"

"I broke it, I was clumsy. I knocked it off in the dark last night."

She'd put another by Davy's bed, an extra, which had been in the guest room.

"What a pity!" Helen said. "That was such a pretty pair." She added hopefully, "Maybe you'll find another to match it."

"I doubt it," said Meg. "I'll start looking again for a milk-glass pair, but I might have to settle for satin glass."

She thought: I'll use the guest-room pair in here and put mine there. She did not want the lamp which had survived, to remind her.

Rhoda gave her party . . . all the neighbors she'd met were there, also her house guests, a couple named Lorsen, from Denver, and a cousin and his wife from New York. Hal asked a couple of boys from college, who lived at a distance, and were visiting around. It was a gay, comfortable evening.

Standing at the buffet table, talking to several people, Davy saw Bob making his way toward him. Bob picked up a plate and commented, "So much food. A feast for Belshazzar."

"It's good food," Davy said. "I'm having seconds, as a matter of fact. What happened to you? You're usually first in line."

"Too much going on; my gastric system can't take it. One thing I'm grateful for, I don't go in for office parties, my own or anyone else's."

"My outfit does," Davy reminded him, "but enough in advance to allow the participants to recover in time for Christmas at home."

Bob helped himself to several things. Without enthusiasm. He asked, "Where's everyone?"

"Here I think. I bet you could shoot a cannon down Main Street and not hit anyone; and through most of the houses, too. If you're being specific, I see your wife talking to our hostess and some others. And Meg's in a corner listening to Maida Waring. There's also a cluster about the bar, and little maids passing swiftly among the revelers with trays and trays and trays. Rhoda's butler's an executive. He directs."

"Well," said Bob, "I'll find a nook and sit; after which I may as well mingle. That's all that's required of us. But I wish I were in bed."

"You've really had too much Christmas."

"I guess so," Bob said. He wandered off, and after a while Davy found himself at a table with Rhoda and the Warings. It was absurd to feel self-conscious. He had not made a move toward Rhoda since she had greeted him and Meg upon their arrival, nor had she singled him out. And why should she?

When they reached home, very late, Meg remarked, "It was a lovely party, really, and everyone seemed to be having such a good time." It was a normal comment, and her only one.

She thought: Tomorrow I'll do something about the lamp.

They went to the holiday dance at the

Club; they went to the Watsons on New Year's Eve, and on January third, Bob was taken by ambulance to the hospital, with what was diagnosed as a coronary occlusion. Mike was in attendance, also a heart specialist from the village, and a consultant from Hartford. No one could believe it — at his age. No one ever believes these things. And they'd seen him so recently — on New Year's Day when the Watsons had stopped by for a moment to inquire: How are your heads?

Meg met Davy at the door when he returned from work and told him. Helen had telephoned Meg from the hospital; she hadn't wanted to call Davy at work.

Davy went into the living room and sat down heavily on the nearest chair without taking off his hat and coat. He said bewildered, "But . . ."

"He seemed so well . . ." Meg said. She was almost crying.

"Come to think of it, he hasn't," said Davy. "Up at the Lake he complained he was tired; and at the Club one night; and at Rhoda's party. . . . Oh, this is a hell of a thing to happen."

"Poor Helen . . ." said Meg. She sat on the hassock by the big chair and laid her head against Davy's knee as Corky so often did. "I'm scared," she murmured.

He knew what she meant: frightened for Bob, of course, and for Helen and the children, but, also for herself and for him. You're always scared when something happens to someone around your own age.

After a while she rose and said, "Better take your things off." He did so and they had a drink — he had several and she made no comment — and then they had dinner, because you always have dinner no matter what happens.

"I don't suppose anyone can see Bob?" Davy asked.

"No; he's in oxygen. Helen's staying at the hospital. Mike managed to get a room for her."

"What about the kids? Shouldn't we take them?"

"I offered, but she'd already sent for her sister — the one in New York; she drove right out."

"I see." He kept thinking of Bob, complaining now and then of fatigue — but everyone does that, including, me, he thought.

"All we can do for them," said Meg, "is pray."

She meant it, he knew. Perhaps it helped her. There were no words in the petition which he formed, not just in his mind or with his lips, but, with his whole being.

Corky came and sat with them; he was sorry, too.

The days went on, and Bob was better; he was out of oxygen and he could have visitors. When Davy saw him, he said cheerfully, "Well, I expected this sometime — but not for another thirty years."

Davy sat in the one comfortable chair and remarked, "So let this be a lesson to you — and to us all."

"What's that mean? Some lesson! Why did I have to be Teacher?"

"Forget it," Davy said. "You'll be out of here soon and then perhaps you'll take Helen and go south and Liz will stay with the kids."

Liz was the sister from New York, the divorced one, whose children were grown. Bob nodded. "We've talked about something like that. Big deal," he added, "staggering through the rest of my days, being spoon-fed."

"But you won't be," Davy argued. "You'll be leading a normal life, just not pressing your luck. You'll get out on the links. . . ." He went on at some length about the normal lives cardiacs can lead, and the mild exercise now so important a factor.

"Oh, sure, Mike's been all over that with

me, and Doc Stein and the other guy. Just let me gripe some, will you? I can't to Helen. Not that she'd mind. She'd listen, but she has enough on her plate just now. As an executor of my will —"

"Oh, shut up," said Davy to his closest friend.

"O.K., O.K. I know all the angles. The heart man — the one from Hartford" — Bob looked mildly pleased — "big shot . . . wait till I get his bill — he gave me the directions, the guidance, the warning, and the you-can live-to-be-ninety bit."

"Mike told me that once," Davy said.

"Probably right," agreed Bob, "but I'd settle for, say, sixty, at this juncture."

A nurse came in, signaled politely at Davy, and he left, deeply depressed. Now he must go home, report, and talk his visit over with Meg.

Since Christmas Eve, and what he thought of as the last-up-to-the-present reconciliation, they'd had neither discussion nor argument. The lamp had disappeared from Meg's bedside table, and the odd one from his; the pair from the guest room took their places. And since Bob's attack she had . . . the word was "clung." Sometimes he thought she found a morbid sort of satisfaction in discussing phases of Bob's illness, and she saw Helen every day, if only for a moment.

Once he said, "Meg, please try not to surround me with apprehension."

To his astonishment, she smiled and said, "But I always have. Didn't you know that?"

"I certainly didn't or I'd have beaten it out of you. . . . well, perhaps I did, in a way . . . vaguely."

"And don't tell me it's negative thinking!"

"Isn't it?'

"Maybe. I don't know. It's just — natural. You and Bob are the same age."

"So are countless millions of other people, dear."

She didn't answer that. She just said, "I don't see how Helen stands it."

"Helen would. We all know that." He didn't, as did most of their mutual friends, marvel at Helen's stamina and calm. He thought he knew her. In a way Helen and Rhoda were not unlike; outwardly dissimilar they both had, he believed, an inner strength.

Meg spoke of Rhoda now as if she had tuned in to his mind; as a matter of fact, she often did. She said, a trifle jealously, "Rhoda's been wonderful to Helen — to Liz and the kids, too."

She had been: sending her car and chauffeur so that Helen need not drive; sending books to Bob, and flowers from her small greenhouse when he was allowed to have them; seeing that Cora got to dancing class and Laurie and Peter to their various routine projects, when Liz was busy; and always asking if she could do errands.

Davy recognized the little spark of jealousy. It was part of Meg's nature. A possessiveness, which extended even to her friends.

He said, "Rhoda understands the situation."

"We're not exactly ignorant of it," she reminded him.

"No, of course not, but she's been through all this."

"Oh? I'd forgotten. What did her husband die of?"

He answered quietly, "A heart attack, but that's not to say that Bob will."

He did, however, during a second attack, shortly before he was due to leave the hospital.

Everyone helped Helen; everyone did, as the phrase runs, all they could. Liz wanted to take the children to New York with her, but Helen said no. It was best for them to be with her. Peter, the oldest, was in something close to a state of shock. Even with Liz there, Helen had her hands full with all three, and having her hands full was her job.

Rhoda met Davy the day before the funeral on the street in the village. They went to the shop on the corner for coffee. She said thoughtfully, "The excitement keeps you doing the things you must do; in Helen's case her three children, in mine Hal — but he was older. After a while you come alive again and that's pretty bad. I wish I could do more for her, but kind as everyone is, she'll have to do most of it alone, by herself. There are times when she'll wish she didn't have the children, just so she could creep off somewhere and beat her head against a wall; but, mostly, she'll be profoundly grateful for them — as I am for Hal."

Davy went home thinking of Meg. If anything happened to him . . . what a stupid euphemism! . . . well, then — if he died . . . there were no children.

At the church he and Meg sat in back of Helen, the children, and the few members of her family and Bob's. He wondered why she had permitted the children . . . but that was up to her. After the service as they rose, he saw Meg looking at Helen as she went quietly down the aisle, her arm around Laurie.

He thought that, as long as he had to live,

he would never forget Meg's expression. It was one of pure envy.

Davy felt physically ill. Meg, in her dark dress and coat, her small black hat, stood quietly, her arm touching his. She had been crying and her cheeks were still wet. But, now, she was actually looking at her dearest friend — a widow — with envy. It was still in her eyes when she turned to him as they prepared to leave the pew. It was not that Davy could read all facial expressions as gypsies do tea leaves, but there are some which anyone can identify: sorrow, fear, love, tenderness, hate, anger . . . the undiluted emotions; and in this instance envy. He had, a few times in their married life, seen Meg look with envy at someone, or something.

Why now?

Walking with her in the sober procession, her thought communicated itself to him in essence. It was simple enough: Now, Helen, although she has her sorrow, has Bob — signed and sealed, forever her own. Helen possessed her husband, safe.

As Meg walked down the aisle with Davy, her eyes filled again with tears, which was natural, the Joneses and the Watsons being the closest of friends. She was thinking: If it were Davy . . . ? She was also thinking that, if ever she could know she had him —

safe — she could forget. Perhaps, instinctively, she knew that we tend to deify the dead.

Meg and Davy returned to the Watson house with the relatives and a few other friends after the services in the cemetery. Helen's sister had reached home ahead of them and was there with the children who had not gone to the cemetery.

Everyone said Helen was marvelous. Meg said it to Rhoda, who nodded and commented, "Most of us are, you know, for a while at any rate. What people don't know is that you aren't around, really. You go through all the motions, you walk and talk, and do the things expected of you. But you aren't there." She added that she had been touched to know that Helen wanted her, a new friend, to be here, and then said, "Perhaps, later, I'll be able to help her."

Everyone tried, each in his own way, to help Helen. She knew it and was grateful, but she was preoccupied with the children's needs, their emotional reactions and the family situation generally. She saw Davy alone; he and Seth Adams, Bob's partner, were executors. They had long, private talks, not wholly about the estate.

Helen would be reasonably well off. Bob had believed in insurance; the house was free and clear; there were policies which would give the children adequate educations, and from the time he'd earned his first dollar — not, it seemed to his wife, so very long ago — he had systematically saved and invested.

CHAPTER 12

At dinner with Meg and Davy one evening in the early spring, Helen said, "You've realized, of course, that I can't go back to the Lake this year?"

Meg said, "Yes. We talked it over and we thought you wouldn't. That's why we haven't said anything to you about it."

"I'd like to in a way," Helen said, "but I'm afraid it's something I can't take; not yet anyway. Perhaps another year — but just now . . . the associations —" Her voice broke, a little. She added, "Bob would understand. I'm sure he does."

Yes, Davy thought, he'd understand.

Bob Watson had been greatly liked, and now he was greatly missed and mourned, but life is an escalator, moving on, always, and once Helen said to Rhoda, "I suppose pretty soon I'll stop having nine dinner invitations a week and just become the difficult addition to any family table, the extra woman."

Rhoda agreed. She knew all about that. "There's always a time when people, no matter how fond they are of you, stop being sorry for you," she commented.

Davy and Meg discussed their own summer plans; they did not want to return to the Lake either . . . even if they could. By this time the cottage probably had been rented, anyway. Davy had notified the owner of Bob's death and had said he doubted they'd renew. Now he suggested they might stay home for a change, take little trips, midweek, rather than weekends, run up to New Hampshire, even Maine. Or would Meg prefer a couple of weeks in Nova Scotia?

She said she wouldn't. "If we stay home," she reminded him, "you can get things done about the house."

He made a face at her; he was not particularly good with his hands, not a tenth as good as she was.

In the end they decided to stay home and, if they wanted a trip, to play it by ear. Earlier in their married life, before they had moved here and started going to the Lake with the Watsons, they'd spent vacations in just that unplanned way. In the city, with little money to spend, they had gone to park concerts, taken bus rides, and found a thousand and one things to do, spontaneous and fun; they'd even managed an occasional weekend in the country. Today there were more places to go and they decided to take their chances.

This year, as it happened, Davy's vacation would fall earlier than usual — in July. He found himself wondering if Bob could have taken that time off too?

When Meg and Davy were at Rhoda's one night for dinner, he spoke to her about Bob. He was standing with her on the terrace, a little apart from the others. He said, "A man's life is like a stone . . . when it's flung into the pond, the water closes over it, there's a splash, then widening circles and presently ripples on the shore and, after that, everything's quiet again."

"Yes," Rhoda said, "I know. But you mustn't resent it. I did; perhaps I still do, but I try not to."

Meg came over with a glass in her hand. "What are you two arguing about?" she asked.

"We aren't; we're agreeing," Davy said.

"How nice," Meg commented politely. She smiled at her hostess and went away again.

It was a very hot summer, with high humidity. Before July came, Corky panted in the yard beneath the trees, or lay under the dining room table, or on the flagstones of the small terrace and looked at them with reproach. Hal Howard was off with a group

201

of boys to Europe and Rhoda often asked Meg and Davy to the house. She was a woman who seemed happiest when she had a number of people about her, which Davy thought was odd. She lacked the drive, the vivacity, the fever of the dedicated hostess; he did not think her innately gregarious. He decided, however, that she enjoyed people, but quietly, and that no matter how many were with her, she could, at any time she wished, withdraw into some central secret citadel of her being.

Sometimes she came to their house, often alone, and as they were becoming "old friends," she helped Meg in the kitchen. Rhoda was, they discovered, to their astonishment, a gifted cook, and the three of them, sometimes with Helen as a fourth, had supper on the terrace when the nights cooled off enough to make it pleasant.

Meg said restlessly one evening, "What a summer! I can't bear it; and it's not even the end of June." She pushed her hair back in her personal gesture of defeat.

"You aren't going away, are you?" Rhoda asked.

"Oh, just here and there," Meg answered vaguely.

Helen was with them that evening. She sat with her arms behind her head and looked toward the horizon. She had lost weight; she was quieter. She still laughed, and made her little jokes and as Davy once remarked to Meg, sometimes rattled on almost, but not quite, in her old way. Now she announced that she'd finally made up her mind she'd take the children to visit her aunt — and, of course, Bob's people — in California. The children had always wanted to go. "Peter and Cora were with us that time, ages ago," she said, "but Laurie hadn't been born then. She always felt cheated; and the others really don't remember too much. And now, there's Disneyland."

"How you going?" asked Davy.

"Station wagon."

Davy was appalled. "But that's a terrible drive, Helen!" he expostulated.

"I know, but we'll take it in easy stages. . . . The cat will live with Mrs. Lowry. She loves her."

"But, still —" Davy began.

"We'll stop, short of dark, every day," she promised, "and stay somewhere overnight. The kids look forward to it and they're easy to travel with. Bob taught them to travel well. . . ."

Her voice trailed off. She thought: Just to get in a car and drive . . . and drive . . . and drive. She looked up and, in the light of the hurricane candles, saw Rhoda's regard fixed upon her with understanding and compassion, and thought: What a nice woman she is. What a dear person.

So that was the Joneses' stay-at-home summer and whether it would have been better, worse, or as bad, to go away somewhere, perhaps to a new resort, Davy didn't know. At the Lake — and before the Lake — he'd always had plenty to do, to amuse and distract him. This summer there seemed no point in getting up in the morning — except that it was too hot to stay in bed — and even less in going to bed. He puttered about the yard and house, played golf, took Meg for the short trips they'd talked about . . . a lake here, a hill there, motels, inns, drives around the countryside.

They appeared to have settled into an armed truce. Meg's clinging and the aggressiveness which had so startled him were gone. He now had a remarkably pretty, amiable, and quite capable wife, who went places with him, kept their house, entertained — and stayed her distance. When upon occasion he tried to recapture, if only briefly, something of that which once they'd known and in which they had rejoiced, she made the inevitable excuses: She was tired, or her head ached. Sometimes, quite frankly, there was no excuse — just, "No, Davy." On other occasions she submitted. He could feel her resignation.

"What has happened to you — to us, Meg?" he asked one night.

"I don't know," she said listlessly. And then, the old refrain, "I'm sorry."

She knew well enough. She suffered from a corroding shame, remembering herself not long ago, telling herself miserably: It was just that I was trying. Trying what? To get him back again, she assured herself, but she knew better than that. She knew that, actually, she had never lost him. It was she herself who was lost.

They talked, of course; they watched a screen at home or in a motion-picture house. They listened to music, good, bad, and indifferent, and were glad when they went to see people or people came to see them because then, afterwards, they had more to talk about. Now and then, if it wasn't too hot, she walked around the golf course with him. Occasionally he played with Rhoda, whose club membership had been, as Meg expressed it, "jammed through." On one afternoon, when Davy was laughing with Rhoda, standing by the bench at one of the holes, waiting for Meg to catch up, he saw with a pure pang of grief her determined, flushed face, her hair damply curling about her forehead. Her mouth was set, as if she were clenching her teeth, but as she reached them, she smiled and said, "I can't keep up with you two."

Davy was not stupid; he knew that Meg was afraid of Rhoda because she was a lovely woman, unattached, and warm and kind as well. But there was nothing he dared say; he could not expose Meg to herself — nor could he give himself away. She would deny the fear, or if she did not, then he would have to begin the denials.

During this vacation Amy turned up and stayed a few days. Corky immediately went upon his best behavior. He did not like Amy, but he respected her; also, he felt she respected him; he did not closely approach her. You might say, they bowed as they passed, or that Amy bowed and Corky lifted his topper.

"How do you manage with Corky in a motel?" she asked.

"Some places take dogs; and he's a good traveler," Davy said.

"But you could leave him at the vet's."

"He isn't happy there," said Meg.

"Well, it takes all kinds . . ." said Amy. "If you'd told me that you weren't going to the Lake, I would have asked you to stay with us."

"Maybe," Meg suggested, "if your house isn't too bulging at the seams, I could come later by myself? After Davy's vacation, I mean. I'm sure he can get along without me," she added evenly.

Davy said he'd get along.

"Good," said Amy. "When I get home, I'll take a look at my wretched calendar and see what Edwin's doing and where the kids will be. I need a social secretary to keep track of them."

Her expression altered very slightly. Meg, who happened to be looking at her, felt that a light had been turned on. She remembered when Amy, recovering from surgery, had engaged a secretary to help with her heavy correspondence, the requests for donations, the excuses incidental to her illness, and then had kept her on because she was so clever about keeping Amy's and the children's engagements straight . . . all the various classes, the meetings, the committees, the back and forth to schools. Meg couldn't remember her name; she did recall her as small and slight, not pretty in the least, but soft-spoken and pleasant. . . . So that was when Edwin, "feeling neglected," had found feminine companionship near at hand!

Before Amy left she took Davy off, alone, and said, "I hope you'll let Meg come to me for as long as she wants to stay . . . next month maybe? It's up to her. I'm free enough or can make myself so. I didn't suggest any dates, when she spoke about it; I was afraid she'd think me too eager."

She paused, as if waiting for a comment, or question, but Davy raised his dark eyebrows and said merely, "My dear Amy, I wouldn't think of trying to keep her home."

"She looks dreadful," said Meg's sister, "and she's so jumpy. I've never seen her that way before — at least not for some time. You haven't been quarreling, have you?"

Davy laughed. He said, "Quarreling? Nothing could be more remote, Amy. We get along superbly — Darby and Joan."

"You needn't —" she began but broke off as Meg came into the room and then went on smoothly, ". . . manage all right, can't you?"

"Manage what?" Meg inquired, a basketful of flowers on her arm. "Are you two hungry? I'm just going to arrange these and then I'll start supper."

"Let's go out," Davy said. "How about the Club? It's hotter'n Tophet here tonight; it might be cooler there. Anyway, it will be a change."

"All right," said Meg, and then: "Manage what, Amy?"

"Without you. I was talking about your projected visit, if Davy can really spare you."

"He'll get along fine," said Meg, expressionless. "He isn't a bad cook, you know. There'll be Mrs. Lowry for essentials and Corky for companionship and always, now that he gets away from work a little earlier, golf."

"That's right," said Davy. "When do you girls want to eat? I'll phone for a table."

Later, as they went out, the women in short, cool frocks, Davy looked closely at Meg and did not think she looked dreadful. She looked, as a matter of fact, very well.

Rhoda was at the Club with a group of people at a big table. Meg and Davy waved to her and as they reached their own corner. "Who's that?" Amy asked. "I never saw her before, and I thought I knew all your crowd. Is she someone's guest?"

"I told you all about her," Meg said. "That's Rhoda Howard. She's been here — almost a year, isn't it, Davy? She has the old Crosswell place. We see a lot of her and like her very much."

"Yes," Davy answered, "she's a fine person."

"What's her status?" Amy inquired.

"Widow," said Davy. "One son." And Meg added brightly. "Denver. Very social and tons of money."

"What does she do?" Amy inquired. She was always interested in what people did. If she were keeping the celestial accounts, she'd put down first who you were (that is to say, who your antecedents were) and then what you did.

"Oh, nothing," Meg answered. "Why should she?"

"I was thinking of civic interests," Amy said severely.

"Well, she's on one of my committees," Meg explained, "and I think she does some volunteer work in the hospital."

"That's better," said Amy. "I disapprove of people who merely write checks."

Davy said pleasantly, "She hasn't always been as useless, if that's what you're thinking, Amy. She and her husband practiced law together before his death."

"Since Bob's death," Meg said, "people have been urging Rhoda to return to practice. Of course, she'd have to pass the state bar examinations, but I doubt that would be a problem."

Davy was astonished; it was not rare nowadays for Meg to astonish him. He said,

"I didn't know that, Meg."

"Rhoda just told me the other day. She won't hear of it."

"The town could use another good lawyer," Davy observed.

Meg shrugged her pretty, tanned shoulders. She'd been going to the beach a good deal this summer. She said, "Well, she doesn't have to, naturally, and apparently she feels under no obligation."

A waitress brought their drinks and Amy remarked, "Judging from this distance, I wouldn't bet she'd stay a widow long. Of course, there aren't many eligible men around here."

Meg ticked them off on her dainty fingers: Mr. Koren, who was eighty; Fred Hummock, three times divorced; a few young men between twenty-five and thirty, and not many of those; and naturally, kids the age of Rhoda's own son.

"But then," she ended, "there are always other women's husbands."

"*They're* eligible?" Amy inquired with lifted brows.

"Not in your sense, of course," Meg admitted, "although sometimes they can be made eligible. But, there's always fun and games."

Amy looked sharply at her sister. That

remark — that light, quick glancing blow —
wasn't like Meg. Amy thought: Has Davy
. . . ? And then, horrified: But I warned her;
I did my best to warn her.

She thought, but did not say: I'd like to
shake some sense into her. Well, perhaps
when she comes to me, she'll open up and
talk, really talk.

CHAPTER 13

Davy's vacation ended and he returned to work with an enthusiasm which was unusual following a holiday. Usually, he had griped gently about it — to Meg or the Watsons; even to Corky, a patient listener up to a point. He'd say, "Siberia, here I come," or, "Suppose I'd been born with twenty million. I wouldn't have to work, ergo, I wouldn't have to go back to it." On one such an occasion, Bob had reminded him that there's no harder work than having money, especially that which you haven't earned . . . keeping, spending, or just watching it. But this year — even with the continuing heat and vacationing people sending idiotic cards, even with the difficult new salesman, for Dick Norton had to go, after all — Davy liked being back in the office. He even made do with a Miss Vaughan, as his invaluable Mrs. Easton's vacation had been extended because of a parent's illness.

There was no need to ask himself why? He knew why.

At least the atmosphere in the office was clear as well as air-conditioned, and the people he saw every day and with whom he talked were real; he saw them standing, walking, sitting. Meg, he couldn't see, or, only in outline. It was as if, when he was home, or with her anywhere, he groped through fog. He'd been in heavy fogs, once at Cape Cod years ago, and again in Nova Scotia when he was on a holiday from college. Men who had been in London during the war had spoken to him of people looming up eerily, in fog and blackout; you knew they were there, but you couldn't see them. He couldn't see Meg either.

They talked of Helen, who was getting ready for her trip to California, and Davy told Meg about Dick Norton, whom she knew. "Bemis left the firing to me," he said. "He would. The day before he went on vacation he called me in . . . this wasn't really a personnel matter, so he didn't say anything to Harkness except that I'd push the switch."

She was mildly interested. He expected no more. After all the dismissal was hardly world-shaking, except to Dick and his family. He thought: I think I can get him a job, one for which he'll be temperamentally suited. He did eventually, and the phoning and the writing took up some slack.

In August, Meg left for Amy's. On the morning of her departure in the station wagon, she tweaked Corky's silken ear gently, said, "Look after Davy while I'm away and be a good boy," and then kissed her husband on the cheek. He reflected that both these demonstrations sprang from the same source: habituated affection. "Now, behave yourself," she added and whether she spoke to him or to Corky he wasn't altogether sure.

Meg was fond of, and good to, Corky, but to her he was a dog and not, as to Davy, a person of spirit and dignity, who happened to have four feet.

Up until one spring — so long ago, he thought — he'd been — upon the rare occasions when Meg went away without him, usually to Amy's — almost intolerably lonely and restless, and the house had become unpleasantly empty . . . but, not now. This emptiness was good; so was the freedom; he came and went as he pleased; ate when, where, and what suited his current fancy. All this he'd done upon the other occasions, but hadn't liked it. Now, he did. At the office there were problems demanding extra concentration; and with Bemis away, more work fell to Davy's lot than usual. He almost embraced Mrs. Easton on her return, as the IN basket, despite Miss Vaughan's diligence, was a nightmare.

Once he went on a short, very hot trip, stayed overnight, and rose before dawn to get back to the plant. Every evening, he dutifully telephoned Meg; sometimes she and Amy and Edwin, were out; so he left a message. Everything was fine at home, he said to whomever had replaced Matilda. He noticed without astonishment or resentment that Meg did not call him back.

A golf game was easy enough to pick up; and the days were long with daylight saving. Often, he left the office, played golf at the Club and had dinner there. He played with Rhoda several times and returned to her house with her, after a shower and change, to have a drink on the terrace. They talked together easily, of nothing profound; theater, books, politics, the altering pace of the very small planet upon which they lived. He always went home refreshed. Rhoda Howard rested him: her quiet voice, her avoidance of sudden gesture and the emanation of tranquility, the aura of intelligent calm which surrounded her and, of which, from the first, he'd been aware.

Once he asked her a personal question. He had not spoken intimately to her since Christmas and this was, in effect, upon the same subject. He said, "I know this is probably impertinence, but have you ever

216

thought of remarrying?"

After a moment she said, "Sometimes . . . recently. No one, at least of my age, looks forward to traveling the road alone. Sam wouldn't want me to, and Hal will soon be gone. After college there'll be a career for him of some kind. He hasn't made up his mind yet. Not the law; he doesn't want that. It's business administration he's after. Your children," she said smiling, "are lent to you for just a little while." Chin in hand, she sat looking across the terrace to the gardens; roses were still abundant, the annuals very bright, the trees heavy with foliage, but everything, despite constant watering, looked tired and a little dusty.

"No, you shouldn't be alone," he agreed.

"I couldn't marry merely for companionship," Rhoda said, "and I haven't fallen in love — not that I'd expect to as once I did; nothing is exactly repeated, which is not to say a second marriage couldn't be good." An expression which was pure radiance briefly illuminated her face and eyes and then she said again, "No, you can't repeat. But living is, I think, mostly compromise in many ways for any adult. . . . And you never get precisely what you want for the price you are prepared to pay."

Davy was seized with an almost ungovernable impulse to tell this quiet woman what was in his mind and heart and, having told her, ask: How am I supposed to live with myself, and with Meg? What is the compromise there?

He said, "Compromise? Yes, of course." He put down his glass and looked at Rhoda. His eyes, she thought, were as nearly black as human eyes could be and they blazed with purpose. "Meg and I —" he began.

"Please don't, Davy," she said.

"Don't what?" he asked, the impulse choked.

"Don't tell me anything important about Meg and yourself. That is what you were going to do, wasn't it? You weren't just going to tell me how you and Meg had worked out the usual compromises common to any marriage."

"No . . . I thought . . ." He began to stammer slightly, "I — I hoped, you m-might advise me."

"I've advised a great many people," she said somberly, "in my professional capacity . . . and also, some of my friends. But confidences from a friend concerning someone else, also a friend . . ." She shook her dark head. "No, Davy, I'd rather not hear them. I appreciate your wanting to tell me, but you see, I know and like you both very much

. . . if not," she said with absolute honesty, "equally. It's difficult for me to feel close to Meg — as I do, for instance, to Helen, whom I've known for the same length of time. Meg keeps herself to herself. Actually I've always had more men friends than women. I enjoy their minds and their companionship. But — forgive me — whatever is troubling you in your relationship — and it must be that; childless people your age rarely ask advice about anything else — I don't want to know about it. It would put me in an awkward position with Meg and with you, too, for sooner or later you'd regret telling me."

"No," he denied, a little sullenly.

"You can't be sure."

He went away shortly thereafter, with a feeling of frustration followed by relief. Rhoda was right. Better keep some things to yourself, no matter how much you felt you needed the relief of confiding. He had never ceased to regret going to see Herbert Carstairs. Every time he saw the minister — after church, or socially — he felt the older man's unspoken questions.

When Davy reached home that night, he took a steak from the freezer and, while it was defrosting, invited Corky for a long walk. Corky was helpful. He demanded nothing; you didn't have to tell him anything, but should you feel moved to do so, he'd listen awhile.

Davy wondered, as he strolled, what Meg and Amy were having to say to each other?

Could he have known it, the answer was: For a time, not much. Meg enjoyed the big house, the air conditioning, the constant coming and going of the children. They were fond of her and flattered her with attention. She went with Amy to garden parties, committee meetings, a tea, a cocktail party. In the evenings, if Edwin wasn't too tired, they went to someone's house or had people in. They saw a movie or two and went to summer theater. During the second week, on a night when Edwin wasn't home for dinner, Amy said, "He'll kill himself. He could take regular vacations, not just weekends or a fast trip, or a cruise every other year." They were sitting on the terrace and now she asked suddenly, "How are you and Davy getting on?"

"Oh, as usual," Meg answered lightly. "We go out, see people, eat together."

"How about sleeping together?" her sister asked bluntly.

Meg said, "I don't refuse."

"Cold comfort," Amy remarked. After a moment she said, "I advised you once not to do anything drastic. I'm not so sure about that now. You're both young, and unless you can return to a — well — different basis of mutual living" — she broke off and contemplated the end of her cigarette before she crushed it out in an ash tray — "it won't be much of a life . . . just, barring accidents, a long one presumably."

Meg said, "I told you I had no intention of divorcing Davy. I don't believe in divorce."

"Nor do I," said Amy, "but there are times when it could be the lesser of two evils. Besides, you don't have to divorce him, Meg. There's always separation, and until one or the other of you — or both for that matter — wished to remarry, the divorce question needn't arise."

"I haven't considered separation," said Meg. "We go along all right as we are."

Well, Amy thought, she'd done her best to point out, all along the way, the errors and the danger. She'd tried to put into Meg's hands the materials for mending marriage, and apparently she'd failed. It would be pleasant, of course, to have Meg with her for longer than an occasional visit. Amy knew, concerning herself, what other people did not; she was a lonely woman. She'd done her own mending skillfully; it scarcely showed. She and Edwin knew exactly how they stood and on what ground. The children were grown, or almost so. They came and went, like birds. She had succeeded in subduing, on the surface, her passionate maternal instinct; its chief expression was domination, but of this she was not aware. And she'd have to wait awhile before she could unleash the instinct somewhat, and carefully, to include grandchildren. But her relationship to her children did not preclude loneliness. So if, eventually, Meg should come to live with the Masons, Edwin would make no protest; he'd probably be delighted, she thought, wryly. Then she would have the doll with whom she had once played, which once she had totally owned but now was able to detach from her present surroundings for brief periods only. And Meg would be such a help in the household, and with Edwin, as the third at a dinner table, a fourth for bridge. Or if anything happened to Edwin . . .

"You must, of course, do as you think best, and as you wish," Amy said. "But if you ever change your mind, you know you have a home with me as long as you want it, as long as you live."

Meg's eyes filled. She wanted to put her head on her sister's shoulder and cry, without shame, as she had when she was little.

But she was, she assured herself, no longer a child. She pinned on a smile and said, "Yes, Amy, I do know, and I'm really very grateful."

"Mind you," Amy said sharply, determining to be just — was she not always just? — "I still feel you have made too much of something trivial, something without importance, and the longer you maintain this attitude, the more difficult it will be to make your marriage work."

Meg was silent, looking away into the dark brilliance of the night where fireflies wove their sudden patterns in the trees and bushes. If, as she believed, Amy had accepted her own similar situation and gone on from there, she felt nothing but admiration and envy for her. Amy was an admirable woman, and a strong one. But Amy had children. Meg had nothing which belonged to her marriage except Davy, as she'd told him once. Whether you leave a person for twenty minutes, an hour, or thirty years, isn't the point, she thought. It's the leaving, itself . . . the betrayal, the treachery, in this case the careless tearing apart of the fabric of a marriage which she had believed indestructible.

They heard the telephone ring and presently a maid came to say that Mr. Jones was calling Mrs. Jones. This was a new, an older, woman, not the pretty Matilda whom Meg had known, or even her replacement. For the replacement, too, Amy said, had married. Meg thought, smiling to herself, of what Amy had said when she came this time. "I don't know what's gotten into them," she'd remarked; "they all bounce off and get married!"

"I'll be right there, will you tell him, please?" said Meg, and rose without haste. And Amy said, "Davy's very" — she almost choked swallowing the accustomed word "faithful," and ended instead, "attentive."

"Yes, isn't he?" Meg agreed. She went to talk with Davy and returned shortly.

"How are things on the home front?" Amy asked.

"As usual . . . the latest office wrinkles have been ironed out, Corky's fine, Davy's had one spell of indigestion and a couple of swims at the beach; he plays golf . . . he said he played with Rhoda today."

"Rhoda? . . . Oh, the woman I saw at the club?"

"Yes."

All Amy said was, "She's most attractive."

"We think so," said Meg.

"Let's go in," Amy suggested. "There's no point in waiting up for Edwin or the children."

The children were all at a dance.

A few days later, when Meg was leaving, Amy came out to the car with her. There was no one about but the young people on the tennis court some distance away and the gardener's helper, whirring along on a lawn mower.

The two women kissed, said the usual things, and Meg got into the car. She had not started it when Amy leaned in at the window.

"Margaret —" she said.

Her eyes were wide with anxiety, Meg saw, and with some other emotion which she could not identify. Before Meg could speak Amy said, low and hurried, "There's something I haven't told you — he wouldn't want me to, he made me promise not to —"

"Who wouldn't want you to tell me what?" asked Meg, disturbed. "What is it, dear?"

"Edwin. It's his heart . . . he's had a couple of minor attacks . . . remember I wrote you; I said he had a virus? But these attacks could be the forerunner of something serious. And he works too hard, no matter what the doctors say."

Meg said inadequately, "I'm so terribly sorry." She was. She liked Edwin and for a moment her affection for him and the shock of the disclosure overrode her feeling for

225

Amy. Then she said, "If there's anything I can do . . . ?"

"Nothing now," Amy said. "Just stand by, will you?"

Meg drove away. It was hard to think of Edwin, astute and kind, a man who drove everyone including himself — but excluding Amy and the children — as an invalid, even a semi-invalid. On the other hand, she reflected, as the car ran smoothly toward home, it's not difficult to imagine Amy as an efficient figure in a sickroom, home or hospital . . . one who spoke in a clear voice, but lowering it as she would the blinds; who managed nurses without antagonizing them. Meg knew from experience, for Amy had taken over the nursing of her small sister on many occasions, and later had done the same for her own children. She could be soothing, she could be firm, she could be unexcitingly amusing — she could be anything the occasion demanded. And, Meg thought further, it was not hard to visualize her sister as a widow, either, continuing to live as she had lived, ordering her affairs and those of her children — being busy.

A wave of shame and pity invaded Meg and she thought: How cold-blooded! How could I ever think such a thing?

She reached home in good time, shortly

before Davy did. She had leisure to unpack, bathe, and dress and when he came in, she was brushing her hair.

He'd suggested that he take her to the Club for dinner — it remained the best, if not the only place in town — and her short printed chiffon dress, not new but one he liked, lay on the bed.

"Hi," he said, constrained. The woman in the mirror, whom he saw the moment she saw him, was a stranger, with a face as smooth and closed as a bud, and blue-gray eyes intent upon the smoothing gestures of the brush.

"Hi, yourself," Meg said. She turned on the dressing table bench and offered her cheek. He ignored it and kissed her mouth, a glancing kiss and she thought with despair that he still had, and probably would always have, until her blood ran thin and cool, the power to disturb her. But she would not accept such a reaction as important; no surface response ever is she thought as he turned away. Then she saw her own face in the mirror, startled, a little pale. . . .

But that was what Davy had been trying to tell her all these months, and Amy, too, in her way: the surface response was of no moment.

That was different, she assured herself.

Davy sat down on a low chair nearby. He said, with an effort, "I missed you." It wasn't true, he hated saying it and was relieved when Corky came galloping in, all feathers flying, to repeat the welcome he'd given Meg when she entered the house.

"That'll do, silly," said Meg and patted his head.

"He was lost without you," said Davy, also untruthfully. Corky was devoted to Meg; he missed her, probably more than Davy had, but he could manage without her.

"I'm a little late," Davy apologized. "I'll grab a shower and change and then we'll have a cool, easy dinner and talk."

He was appalled to think that, once she had told him everything — or almost everything — that had or had not happened at Amy's, once he'd run through the past mental engagement book with her, there'd be nothing left to talk about.

CHAPTER 14

They were early at the Club, and had a tall, cool drink in the bar before they went to a porch table. Meg had had two drinks, but Davy had three, and she asked, when he had ordered the third, "Isn't that a little excessive?"

"I don't think so," he said carefully. "I'm celebrating your return." He smiled at her; it was easier after the second drink. They went out to the porch. "I asked Jack for a nice table," he said.

Beyond the porch, people were sitting at small tables on the terrace. It was the era of terraces, he reflected . . . everyone, every place, had a terrace; even he and Meg had a small facsimile.

It was still light; late golfers straggled in; people came up to speak to them: Where had Meg been for heaven's sake? Someone said, "I thought you'd left his bed and board."

"Never," said Meg firmly, "that is to say only temporarily. He'll have a hard time getting rid of me unless he strikes me down and buries me in the garden."

Davy said, "Corky would dig you up."

As dinner progressed, she spoke of the things she'd done and the plays she'd seen, one good, one bad — "a tryout, it will never make Broadway" — and of the meetings she'd attended with Amy — "she takes more upon herself all the time; it's rather frightening" — and of the Mason children. Martin was being tutored, part time — he'd failed in one subject; Edwin, Jr., had elected the Air Force; also, he had a girl. Amy liked her, but at this point it couldn't be serious.

"Why not?" Davy asked perversely.

"No reason, I suppose, except the Air Force hitch and all that. Anyway, Amy thinks he's too young." She went on to say that Hilary had an avalanche of beaux, particularly the one she'd met at her roommate's debut. "He can't come to visit her this year; he's a counsellor in camp, or something. He bombards her with mail and telephone calls. Hilary's really very pretty," Meg ended.

"She always looked like you," Davy reminded her.

"A little perhaps, but taller, and better-looking."

Toward coffee she said, after turning it over in her mind, "I'm not supposed to tell you this, for Amy wasn't supposed to tell me . . . but Edwin's had a couple of heart attacks. Remember, he was sick twice, and Amy wrote that he had had some sort of virus?"

"How serious were they?" Davy asked, concerned.

"The doctors said not very, but they were, of course, warnings."

"Well, yes. Lord, I'm sorry." He added absently, "Amy will cope," and looked up quickly to see if he had offended his wife. Apparently he had not, for she answered, "That's what I've been thinking."

As they went out, more people were drifting in and Meg remarked with calculated carelessness, "I don't see Rhoda. . . . I thought she came here a lot, though I wouldn't know why, with that marvelous cook . . ."

"She's visiting on Long Island — the New York cousins — we met them at Rhoda's holiday party, but I can't remember their name. Hal comes home next week and she wants to be at the airport to meet him."

Driving home, Meg asked, not as casually, "You saw quite a lot of Rhoda, didn't you?"

His hands tightened on the wheel and he answered evenly, "I suppose so, in a way. We played golf a few times, I went to the house for drinks afterwards. Once we had a drink at the Club, and once I went there to dinner. I told you about it at the time."

"So you did," she replied, without inflection, and immediately spoke of a letter she'd had from Helen Watson. "I'd asked her to write me at Amy's. . . . Incidentally, there's quite a stack of mail at home."

"You said not to forward anything unless it looked important. Nothing did, except a couple of dividends and I put those in the desk."

"Oh, good . . ."

"How are Helen and the children?" he asked. It was still hard to speak of them without seeing Bob take shape before his inner vision, always laughing a little.

"She says everyone's fine, but that the adjustment is hard for them all, particularly Peter."

"It always is, I guess," said Davy and he thought: Sure it is, not only when someone dies; it can be so when someone is alive and sitting beside you and making familiar sounds and gestures.

After they reached home, they sat outdoors for a while and then went in to look at television. "Nothing much but reruns," said Davy. "You must be tired, Meg. Why don't we turn in?"

She said brightly that she wasn't tired at

all; it hadn't been a bad trip; traffic had been comparatively light; besides, the evening had rested her.

So they watched TV for another half hour; but you can't stay up all night without an excuse although, of course, there was always the late-late show.

When they finally went to bed and he took her in his arms, she sighed a little, but was pleasant enough about it.

To take a woman against her volition — and there are men who find it pleasurable, but Davy was not one of them — is one thing; to take a woman who is, or appears to be, dutifully resigned to what is often called the act of love (though often it is not) is another.

He had been accustomed, after what is known as the original adjustment, to response which, if not passionate, was tender and loving; and that, in the long run, is more durable. Not until after that dreadful April had he known another, almost savage Meg; now she, too, had departed. But "that was in another country: and besides the Wench is dead."

It was, rather, as if Meg were.

They were young people, as time is now measured, on the sunny side of forty; they could reasonably expect, as Amy had indicated to Meg, twenty, even thirty or more years of life together.

He considered that next morning, looking into the shaving mirror; and he thought: *Merciful God!*

Perhaps the prospect would not have been as horrifying had he not loved his wife. He was fully aware of her faults, her flaws, certain insensitivities, even stupidities, as she was of his. But he loved her; not loving her, merely accepting her in affection, the years ahead would have been simple if tedious.

This situation was not to be endured, he thought, putting down the razor. Perhaps a clean break . . . ?

What break is ever clean? There are always jagged ends, the roughening, the splinters.

Perhaps there were numberless contented men, completely adjusted to living with a dutiful, pretty wife, who cooked and served an excellent meal, who kept a garnished, attractive house; who welcomed her guests with charm and made a good impression on their friends and on her husband's business associates; a woman who was well liked, who played a fair game of bridge, read the current best sellers and occasionally expressed her own opinion; and who was, as part of the bargain, acquiescent and amiable in the secret passages of love.

Yes, of course there must be many such men, but he was not one of them.

He told himself that he wanted out, at any cost — loneliness, nostalgia, longing, despair, even desolation. He told himself, putting the razor away, that it is entirely possible that the marital relationship — chapter and verse; bell, book, and candle — is artificial. You fell in love, or thought you did; you married soberly, but with an inner radiance and belief, and you lived together until death did you part. But there had to be more than that.

Fourteen years spent in a spotless house and then there is a speck of alien dirt, blown — God knows why or how — by a capricious, brief wind, a south wind, perhaps, sudden and languid. No broom of remorse can sweep that speck away. . . . Oh, it is no longer there in a sense; one cannot see it; no one says: Remember the time when the cleanliness of this house was defiled? . . . But the invisible spot remains; no tears wash it away, no word erases it.

"What kind of a marriage is it," he asked himself, going down to breakfast with Corky, "which, perfect-seeming, is, nevertheless, so easily spoiled."

He thought: I can't face it. I'll love her

until I die. But I *am* dying.

It was not the physical repudiation — though repudiation it was — it was not the absence of the response to which he'd been so long accustomed. It was the gradual withdrawing from him of Meg's inner self, which he thought he knew and now wondered if ever he'd known. It was the remembrance in her eyes, the quick glance, the overt suspicion, the so carefully casual word: "You saw quite a lot of Rhoda, didn't you?" It was the completed barrier between mind and mind, and beyond and above that, between spirit and spirit.

Marriage, he thought — agreeing with Meg that it was a fine day, saying he'd rather have his egg boiled this morning — could be reduced to simple and profound truths . . . in the final analysis, a man and a woman with their backs against the same wall — not one on one side, and one on the other — it is marriage which, at its best, and often at second best, combats the essential loneliness of the individual. Marriage is not only love in every interpretation of the word; it is also, as Rhoda had said of life, compromise, and in a good marriage it is always, no matter what does or does not happen, trust.

Meg said, "I may be a little late tonight. Rhoda's asked a dozen of us for tea."

"All women, I take it," he said mechanically.

"Yes . . . general gossip, tea for those who prefer it, wandering about the garden. It's beautiful now. I never saw such chrysanthemums. She's talking about putting in a pool next year; she says Hal would like it. She also said she'd like our advice, which is one way of being kind — she doesn't, of course, need it. Elsie Masters will be there; she's half out of her mind with envy. Until Rhoda came and put hordes of gardeners to work, Elsie's was the show garden of the town."

"Yes, of course," he agreed. Mrs. Masters was president of the local garden club.

He said, "Well, the evenings are still long and light; I'll find some poor wretch and knock off nine holes before I come home."

"Too bad Rhoda's not free," she said.

Anger was a burning acid in his throat, hot and hurting. He asked harshly, "And what does that mean, exactly?"

"Why nothing. How touchy you are!" She looked at him with surface serenity. "I just meant, you seem to enjoy playing with her."

Under the surface the blue-gray eyes had their special speech. Only the guilty, they were telling him, could be angered by so casual and meaningless a remark.

"Of course I do," he said, and the anger

died, for what was the use? "She plays a good game, better than most women around."

"I'm sure she does," Meg said smoothly. "She does everything well." She thought, with childish ferocity: I could kill her. Of course she does everything well. . . . And I could kill you, too, she thought further, sitting there looking as innocent as the egg you're eating!

"I'm sorry," he said, with an effort, "I didn't mean to jump you."

"That's all right," Meg said. "You've been a little irritable for quite a while . . . the heat and the work, I think . . . and you didn't have a real vacation."

"I had a vacation," he said stubbornly, aware that this was a futile conversation, but unable not to pursue it.

"I meant as we used to have, at the Lake."

She meant with Bob and Helen and their children, with our good friends . . . not last summer; oh, not last summer, but all the summers before.

He said nothing. A thousand vacations — well, twenty, thirty, thirty-five — in the anticipated years of mutual holidays would not suffice him.

He thought: I know she hates me sometimes. But how can I hate her, when I love her?

He wasn't the first man to ask himself that and he wouldn't be the last.

Hal came home from Europe and they saw him next time they had dinner with Rhoda. The boy was brimming with his experiences; he was a happy person; to draw him out was easy. After dinner, they watched the films he'd taken and he said apologetically, "They're not very good. I shouldn't inflict them on a captive audience."

His mother agreed, "Of course you shouldn't," she said, "but I'll probably see them fifty times before you go back to college; still, I'm enjoying them."

"I am, too," Davy said, and Meg murmured politely in the darkness. Watching the sometimes colorful, sometimes blurred, images jerk across the screen, aware of Hal's preoccupation with running the projector, Davy wondered: What is it like to have a son? A son like Sunday's child, good and gay; fun to be with, stimulating to watch. What is it like to recognize your own grave responsibility as a parent? Looking across at Rhoda in the dim light, he thought he could see the amusement, the pride, and the love in her face, and, for just a moment, vicariously, he knew the answers.

When they reached home, Meg yawned. "There's nothing more boring," she remarked, "than amateur movies and slides."

"I liked them," he said rebelliously, and thought: It's too late to be careful, though this is probably leading somewhere; everything leads somewhere now.

It led to her saying, after they'd gone to bed, speaking across the starlit darkness between her bed and his: "You're in love with Rhoda, Davy."

"I am not," he said.

"Yes, you are. I know it." She spoke listlessly, a dark shape in the darkness and then added to his astonishment, "but I don't suppose it matters, since she isn't in love with you."

He said, "Meg, you're really off your rocker."

"She's still in love with her husband," Meg said, as if he hadn't spoken. "When you and Hal were sorting films I went outside with her and we talked . . . I don't know just how it came up. Of course, she won't always be, I suppose." She added, "How long can you be in love with a memory?"

"Some people, forever," said Davy.

"That's morbid," Meg told him, and he recalled her expression in church the day Bob was buried. Was that really how some women felt, envious of an emotionally raw and bleeding widow, because she now possessed her husband in entirety, and always would? Yet there must later be the recognition on the part of the wounded, springing from some deep natural awareness, that wounds heal and — given time and opportunity — not a replacement but a second chance need not be impossible. Rhoda had said that to him, in effect.

"If you died tomorrow," said Meg evenly, "— and you could, of course — I'd remarry, I think, if I had the chance; and, if I died tomorrow, you would, too, like a shot. But I don't expect to die tomorrow any more than you do and if I should, don't set your sights on Rhoda — not for quite a while anyway."

"Meg!"

"Oh, for heaven's sake!" she said. "I'm not accusing you of trying to promote an affair with her. Even if you were contemplating something of the sort, I don't believe you'd get to first base. I'm simply saying that you have some sort of romantic notion about her. You know," she went on, as if confidentially, "it used to frighten me, keep me awake nights and jittery daytimes, when first I realized it. But it doesn't any more. Only," she ended, "don't ever think you can use me for a substitute for something you can't have."

He was greatly shocked. He made no move to go to her, to protest, to try to reassure; all this he'd done on other occasions; now it was simply too late. He said, "I'm sorry you feel like that. I've told you I'm not in love with Rhoda Howard. I'm in love with you."

He lied. He loved her; he could not help himself, it was as much a part of him as the skin on his body, but he was no longer in love. Perhaps, he hadn't been for a long while.

"Oh, that," said Meg; "you're used to me." Then she said something which was unlike her. She said, "I'm sorry I've given you such a bad time, Davy, I tried not to — after a while . . . I honestly tried." She thought of the means she had used and flushed in the darkness. "And I'm certain that everyone we know would agree with you that what you did was of no importance. It's just unfortunate that it was important to me, Davy." Then she said, "If only you hadn't told me . . ."

"I wish to God I hadn't," he said.

"I'm sure of that. Why did you, Davy?" she asked, like a child.

He looked for words and found them without value.

"I told you; I couldn't live with myself; it

had to be a sharing."

"Whatever it was" — her voice was drowsy, trailing off as her physical body pursued the restorative, the brief, the all-too-temporary obliteration of sleep — "it's over. . . . Davy, do you remember the girl we had before Mrs. Lowry?"

"For God's sake," he said, startled and uncomprehending. This was a *non sequitur* if ever he'd heard one.

"Eva, I think . . . yes, that was her name . . . Eva. She broke one of the crystal goblets Amy gave me. She was honest and told me about it, but I was heartbroken. We had twelve goblets — I wonder how many have been broken since; I think we still have eight, I haven't counted — Amy brought them to us from Sweden . . ."

He said, bewildered, "What's this talk about goblets . . . you're half asleep, Meg."

She said, "You told me I could ask Amy if there was an import place in New York and I could replace the broken one . . . I didn't ask her . . . when I saw the pieces . . . shattered . . . shining . . ."

Now he was aware of what she was trying to say. "You can't compare marriage with one of the dozen pieces of glass," he told her.

"Why not?" she asked, momentarily wide awake again. "You can compare it to a thousand things. And if it helps you, Davy, to sit looking dreamily at Rhoda, I don't mind. Perhaps she does — but I don't. I've even thought of looking dreamily at someone myself. But, of course, our motives wouldn't be the same."

"What do you mean, motives?" he asked and was angry again, as angry as he had been in many months.

"I'd just be trying to make you jealous," she explained, "but you're not trying to make me jealous, you're just trying to get away from me, even further. . . ."

She was getting drowsy again, as Davy said, "It isn't I who —"

But she had gone, breathing as quietly as a child, drowned in sleep.

He lay awake for a long time. He would have sworn, not too long ago, that he knew Meg's every reaction even before she reacted. Now he didn't know her at all.

It is customary for the accused to feel guilty, even when he isn't, or assures himself he's not. Davy did not go out of his way to see Rhoda. As a matter of fact, when the leaves had turned, she and Hal had driven into Vermont for a final holiday before he went back to college.

One dazzling morning Davy met her as they both went into the bank. "How about coffee if you have time?" she asked. "The shop's practically empty; too late for breakfast, too early for the first break."

So they went in and sat at a small table and she talked to him about Hal and their trip. And then she said, "Davy . . . please don't be offended . . . but I don't think our golf games, pleasant as they've been, are a good idea."

"Why not? I thought I was teaching you something," he said, warily, waiting.

"When you and Meg came to dinner," she told him, "I talked with her for a while. She seemed interested in my relationship with my husband. Oh, I don't mean that she was prying, but I know something about deviousness and circuitous routes; I've had too many clients not to recognize them. She thinks you're a little in love with me."

He had denied it to Meg and to himself. But now he found himself telling Rhoda the truth. He said instantly, "Why, of course I am!"

Rhoda smiled at him, unstartled, unperturbed. She said, "Thank you . . . but you aren't, really . . . it's just that you aren't happy . . . I don't know what's wrong with your marriage; I don't want to know. You may remember that while Meg was away you started to tell me and I stopped you. I like Meg and respect her. I don't want her hurt. I believe she has been hurt — and I won't be a further cause. I'm fond of you," she said honestly. "I like you as well as any man I've met recently — perhaps better."

He said gravely, "Now I thank you."

She smiled a little. "But, my dear," she said, "I'm not in the least in love with you. You are attractive and I'm aware of it. I'll know I'm old when I no longer experience the normal chemical reactions. . . . Do you know," she added thoughtfully, "I don't believe I'll ever be that old? However, such awareness isn't love, even in its most temperate aspect . . . at least, not for me."

"Rhoda —"

"Wait a minute. It's the beginning of love, of course, but when you have no compulsion to go on from the beginning, why . . ." she shrugged. "I hope I'm making myself clear," she said politely.

"Abundantly," Davy assured her, with very mixed feelings.

"So," she said thoughtfully, "you're unhappy and I'm around; we enjoy the same things and you're attracted to me. Don't mistake it for a *grande passion* or even a little one."

He said, after a moment, "Perhaps you're right. I don't know. I admire you more than any woman I've ever known . . . and I believe love does come into it. Possibly it's loneliness."

"Who isn't lonely?" she asked. "I am, you are, Meg is. It's the natural declension, and ends with 'everyone is,' one way or another. It's a pity you and Meg have no children."

"Yes," he agreed shortly.

"Why didn't you adopt one?"

"Meg wouldn't consider it."

"Of course," she said softly, "flesh of your flesh, bone of your bone, the blood line . . . something like that . . . but we've all known parents of adopted children and their happiness in them. I've steered many adoptions through regular channels."

"Too late now," he said, "even if she'd go along with it." He looked up from the second cup of coffee, cooling in the thick mug. "Rhoda, may I tell you just one thing?"

It was an appeal, a straightforward appeal. And she said, "All right, but — no details."

"S-sometime ago," he began with the sudden stammer, "I-I did something — without reason, logic, thought — and she has never forgiven me." He stopped. "No, that's not true. She forgives me regularly. But she can't forgive — and forget."

"She shouldn't," Rhoda said.

"What do you mean?"

247

"I mean I think one should forgive and remember. If you can remember and, at the same time, forgive, really forgive, you've succeeded in accomplishing — I don't know what to call it — perhaps an emotional overcoming, a spiritual discipline. If you forgive and forget in the usual sense, you're just driving what you remember into the subconscious; it stays there and festers. But to look, even regularly, upon what you remember and *know* you've forgiven is achievement."

"I'll have to think about that," he said.

"Do." She rose. He picked up the check and she said, "I'm late for the beauty shop; you're late for work. My car's parked back of the bank. Good-by, Davy. I'll call Meg soon." She gave him her warm, honest smile and added, "You might do some forgiving too, you know."

"I can't," he said, low, and understood that she had meant, forgive himself.

CHAPTER 15

When Helen Watson and her children returned from California, Meg held open house for all their friends, young and old. The golden weather still held, the children spilled over, out of doors. The Watsons were brown and had put on weight. Peter, his mother told Meg, was more like himself, but Davy thought the boy's eyes were still haunted.

It was at the party that Helen launched her missile. Meg and Davy had known from the day of her homecoming that she was putting her house on the market. She'd give herself ample time to sell it, as Davy had advised her, and then she would move to California, to the pleasant suburb where Bob's family lived, and which was also not far from her aunt. The children were happy out there, she said, and she liked it, too.

Everyone was regretful and that night, after Meg and Davy had cleared up and Corky had crept to bed, feeling his reunion with the Watson children had been too short, Meg remarked that it was as if a link had snapped.

Davy interpreted this as the link with their own mutual past. Bob and Helen had been so much a part of the pattern of their lives; and now they'd be gone: Bob involuntarily, and Helen of her own free will. During the remainder of her stay in the village things would be different; the tenor of the conversations would be, "When I move," or "When you leave."

That would not be for some time, however, as Helen had planned to keep the children in school until June. By then the house would surely be sold, and one would have been found for them in California. Still, her friends would feel that her presence among them was temporary, a perching on the branch, until it was time to migrate.

The following Saturday, Helen and Meg were at the Club, waiting for Davy and Bob's former partner to come in from golf and buy them lunch, and Helen said, looking over the serene, russet landscape, "I suppose I'm chicken and that means immature, not being able to face it here, year after year, as Bob's widow, the extra woman. Possibly what I think of as a new start won't be the solution I now believe it; perhaps making new friends won't be easy — and tearing up roots is a hurt that stays. I don't know that running away is the answer, Meg . . . but when I'm here, I still can't walk down a street without thinking: Perhaps, I'll meet Bob, by accident. And when five or six o'clock comes, I keep listening for a car. It's as if I were in prison, and the front door doesn't open to let me out."

Meg said, "Dear, perhaps if you gave yourself more time — ?"

"How much time? Ten years, twenty?" Helen's round pretty face, tanned, and rosy, was grave. "No, I don't think so — and, if I'm wrong —"

"You can come back," said Meg.

"I can't keep on uprooting the children," Helen reminded her. "They're young; they're going to miss their school and their friends. If it hadn't been for the schools I would have tried to sell the house right away, no matter what Davy and Seth said, but they are all doing so well and I'd like Peter to graduate from junior high here. After that there will be other schools and they've already sworn undying friendships with the kids they've met out there. And while the prospect of no snow appalls them, there's the compensation of living outdoors most of the year. I don't know what Bob would think about this. . . . I expect you'll think I'm crazy, but I pray every night that he knows and approves. . . . Well, it's necessary to

251

make the big decisions, even if they turn out to be the wrong ones."

"It's not that I think you're wrong, just that I'll miss you so much."

"I'll miss you, too. You and Davy will have to take a vacation trip and come see me. I know you don't like planes, but you could fly, for once!"

"I don't think I'd mind now as much as I thought I did," said Meg.

Helen wasn't listening; she was saying thoughtfully, "On the practical side, clothes, all that, it's less expensive in the West. I'm very fond of my aunt. I like the way people live out there and Bob's family are, of course, enchanted that the children won't be far away. . . . I suppose any big city's the same, but the place where we stayed — well, there's less pressure, less hurry . . . and not nearly as much tension."

She paused, and then she said, "I haven't told you what I did the other day."

"What day?"

"The day before your party. Remember you called and there was no answer and when I saw you and you told me you'd phoned, I said I'd been away?"

"Yes, of course." Meg said. Actually she had been curious and a little hurt.

Now Helen said, "I parked the kids with

the Bellows . . . big deal, last cookout and overnight before school opened . . . you know they've youngsters the ages of mine; the boys were going to sleep in a tent, the girls in an attic dormitory. So I just got in the car and went to the Lake. I didn't get back till all hours that night."

"There and back in a day?" said Meg, horrified. "And all alone. Helen, why didn't you ask me to go with you? We could have stopped somewhere overnight."

"Thank you, dear," said Helen. "I did think of it, and I knew you'd come. But it was better for me to go alone, and just — look around. I doubt I'll ever see the place again," she added, trying to be casual, "and it seemed, this time, so queer that's it's un-changed."

"Did you see anyone?"

"No . . . that is, Bill, from the gas station, and I had a sandwich in the corner grocery delicatessen. I knew most of the people we know wouldn't be up there so late; there'd just be the cottagers who come in Septem-ber. I parked back of our cottage — it was empty — and walked down to the shore and sat awhile. . . . So, another bridge burned," Helen said. "Why didn't you and Davy go back this season?"

"We just didn't want to without you."

Helen said somberly, "Wherever you go, it's always without someone — eventually."

The men came trudging up, flushed with exertion and the September sun and after they'd made themselves presentable, they joined Meg and Helen for lunch, on the wide, old porch.

Meg liked Seth Adams. He was a quiet, capable man with humor and under-standing, older than Bob or Davy; forty-five, perhaps. His wife had been an invalid for many years and was now in a wheel chair. Seth was devoted to her, and he went out very little socially. But now that their mar-ried daughter was visiting them, he could take an occasional afternoon off. He was apologizing for his game.

"You did all right," said Davy, "consider-ing you don't get half a dozen games a sea-son."

They knew all about Seth's summers. The Adamses had a spacious place and, fortu-nately, enough money to maintain it. Jessie Adams had a companion-nurse, but when Seth was home they were together; he read to her, played the records she liked, and they talked. In clement weather, he took over from the companion and wheeled Jessie's chair to the patio or down the specially wide path to the gardens. In the summer he had the long, light evenings in which to do so. Because of her situation, he did not take regular vacations — he hadn't since she became ill — only a special day, now and then, or a long weekend. They had a folding wheel chair and a custom-built car, so he could take her driving, but not too great a distance, for she tired easily.

He was talking to Davy now and Meg looked away over the rolling course where the light caught brightly in the water hazards and thought: It must be wonderful to know such devotion.

But no one could wish Jessie out of her wheel chair by the only method she'd ever get out except via the strong arms which now lifted her. She was a patient, prematurely aging woman with great fortitude. She liked people and many came to see her. She had been sustained all these painful, static years. By what, this past decade? Seth's love and acceptance? Jessie never made you feel sorry for her, Meg reflected. Almost every day someone came at teatime — telephoning first to ask if she were up to seeing them — and, often, in the evenings, Seth and Jessie invited people for drinks and conversation. She could live for many years, but if she did not, perhaps Helen and Seth . . .

Meg thought: Why do women always want to matchmake? Why can't they have more sense? But her heart was heavy for her friend, planning the life she spoke of as new but which, essentially, wouldn't be . . . just the old life she might have lived here, but in another setting. Meg thought: Helen knows she's running away. But if you do that, you still have to take yourself with you.

A flicker of pride briefly warmed her; she thought: I wouldn't run away. I couldn't.

It was not until some time later that she asked herself if, actually, she hadn't. There are many routes of attempted escape: California or Hong Kong, sleeping pills or alcohol; and there is always, quite simply, the withdrawal into yourself, like the animal in a cave that cowers against the wall and silently licks its wounds.

This comparison did not occur to her, but she recognized that she was, in effect, trying to escape from Davy. But I can't help it, she told herself in despair.

That evening she stood at the bathroom door talking to Davy as he shaved. They were going to the Millers for dinner and cards. "We'll never get through a hand," she said, resigned. "Mike's sure to be called out."

"Then we'll play three-handed until he

returns . . . or maybe other people have been asked."

"No, Ginger said just us."

Davy put down the razor, ran his hand over his cheek, and twitched a dark eyebrow at her.

"Something on your mind?"

"No, not really. Just Helen." She told him of their conversation and Davy said she shouldn't have gone back to the Lake. "There's no sense in making things harder for herself than they already are."

"I know . . . and she admitted that perhaps, in moving West, she was running away."

"She is."

"I think she's making a mistake," Meg told him.

"Maybe yes, maybe no. If she is, it's her own." He turned and came toward her, bracing a hand against the door, stooping from his considerable height. "Woman," he said, "will you stand away from the door? I have to dress."

"But she knows that running away isn't the solution."

"We're all running away," Davy said, "if not always physically. Fore . . . or gangway . . . or step aside, please . . . or something . . ."

Where is he running to? she wondered. To Rhoda? The name was sharp as a needle in her mind. If not to Rhoda now, to whom else, some other time?

While he was dressing, she thought of the sermon Dr. Carstairs had preached the previous Sunday on the woman taken in adultery. He had said nothing that hadn't been said before from a million pulpits, but he had stated it well.

On the way home Davy had remarked suddenly, "Stripped of all the rhetoric and, yes, even religion, I suppose it boils down to something simple — it takes two to tango."

Within Davy's hearing no one had ever preached on the man taken in adultery. Of course, he thought, the co-responsibility of any man is implicit in "cast the first stone."

Meg remembered that for a moment she had felt strangled, and he had asked quickly, "You all right, Meg?"

"Yes." She had cleared her throat and spoken slowly. "But that was an odd thing for you to say."

"I didn't m-mean to say it," he'd told her. She'd noticed the slight stammer then. "I was j-just thinking out loud."

She'd remarked, looking straight ahead of her, "But I couldn't agree with you more."

That night at the Miller's dinner table, Mike mentioned last Sunday's sermon. He said, "Take my word for it, the old boy's slipping."

"You're hardly in a position to judge," remarked his wife. "You don't go to church three times a year."

"Ah, but when I do, I concentrate. I listen. In my disciplined youth I was dragged by the hand or collar — whichever was handier — so I've heard as many sermons in my time as most men."

"I suppose we all have," said Davy. He was thinking of what he'd said that day on the way home and how white Meg had looked. He'd been a damned fool to say that. But he'd spoken without thinking or, more accurately, had expressed his thought without being conscious of his audience. Now, at his friends' table, he thought of the woman who called herself Vivian. He had not visualized her as a person for a long time. He'd thought of her only as a symbol, or a tool — impersonal as the tool which brings to earth, in ruins, what was once a house. His thoughts amused him, in an unpleasant way: So that's a home-wrecker, he told himself.

"Our first clergyman," Mike was saying, "at least the first I recall — what are you grinning about, Davy, in that sardonic fashion? I'm not being funny, yet —"

"Just at the thought of someone dragging you anywhere, either by hand or collar."

"They still do, metaphorically speaking," said Mike gloomily. "Where was I? . . . Oh, yes . . . the first clergyman I remember — and he lasted some twenty years in the little town where I was brought up — now, there was a fire-eater, an oracle of doom. I used to sit on the edge of the pew — hard and sharp enough to hurt — shuddering with pleasing terror, in much the way kids watch horror pictures today on TV. I'd categorically remember my multiple sins, and wait for the ceiling to crash down around my ears. You, Ginger, you wouldn't know; you were reared half heathen."

"I was not," said his wife indignantly.

"The forensic, frenetic oratory is out of date now," Mike said, "But darned if I don't think most sermons lack something."

"Of course they do," Davy agreed. "This is the era when it's fashionable to go into local, state, and national politics from the pulpit, to say nothing of taking up causes. . . . I don't say this hasn't its place, but that, I think, is in the parish hall."

"Dr. Carstairs' sermons," Meg remarked, "are very spiritual."

"So, they lack punch," said Mike. "I've seen that happen, too. . . . Have some more beef? It's good. . . . Also, the clergy goes all out for lay psychiatry and psychology. I rather expected an interesting disclosure of what motivated the woman taken in adultery — background, environment, family troubles, rejection?" He laughed. "However," he added thoughtfully, "no one ever remarked it might have been fun."

"Mike!" his wife protested.

"Are we grown up or not?" he asked. "No, I assume. Well, all that has its place, too, from the lecture platform, in the discussion group, or in the pastor's study, but not, I contend, from the pulpit. I was pleasantly surprised, but disappointed. I was just about to rise up and make my own diagnosis. I was going to say, 'Bert' — no that wouldn't do — 'Dr. Carstairs, sir, maybe she was hungry?' "

"You're wonderful," said his wife. "Nothing you say makes any sense. But, I enjoy it. . . . There's the phone."

"Damn. . . . Carve your own beef, Davy." Mike got to his feet and seized the extension telephone which sat handily on a serving table. There were extensions in several rooms in this house. He listened. He said, "Yes." Then he barked once or twice and

261

said, "I'll be right along." He returned to the table long enough to spear a piece of roasted potato on his fork, insert it in his mouth, and ask briefly, "What's for dessert? as they say in the commercials."

"Apple pie," Ginger answered.

"Save me a piece. I'll be back 'ere dawn." He grinned at them and was gone. A moment later, they heard a car engine start.

"He doesn't even keep his car in the garage," said Ginger mournfully, "with that beautiful electric-eye door and all."

"I don't know how long he can keep going at this pace," Davy said thoughtfully. He went around to Mike's place, carved himself a slice of beef, and asked, "Seconds, girls? . . . No? . . . Ginger, can't you do something about it?"

"No. When we were married, I swore I wouldn't try to reform him, and I managed to adjust. After all, I knew something of what I was getting into. I worked in his madhouse of an office after I came out of training."

They all heard the mild roar from abovestairs, and she said, "That's Keith. . . . No, Keith and Carl. They're fighting. I'll be right back."

The Miller maid, a distant cousin of Mrs. Lowry's, who was practically everyone's cousin, came in with more vegetables, and Davy said, "This is a wonderful dinner," which pleased her. He thought: Now that Mike and Ginger aren't in the room, we sit here, Meg and I, and haven't a word to say. We might as well be home.

Mercifully, their hostess, slightly flushed and rumpled, returned. She said, "Heaven knows how long Mike will be gone. I telephoned Helen Watson while I was upstairs. If she can get a baby sitter — Peter's out — she'll come round for coffee and sit in for Mike at bridge."

It was a pleasant evening. Mike came in as his guests were about to leave and demanded that they stay for a nightcap. He'd risk one, too, he said; he had extra sensory perception; no one was going to die before the effects of one small highball wore off. But he'd changed his mind about the apple pie.

Going home, Meg said, "Nice time, wasn't it? I like the Millers so much."

"I do, too." Davy said and then he added, "Yes, it was very nice. But we don't have fun together any more, wherever we are, Meg."

"I don't know what you mean," she began. "I just said" — the little fingers of her mind curled delicately away from the challenge;

she would not touch or examine it — "I just said we'd had a nice time."

"Oh, sure, with Ginger and Mike and Helen — but not you with me . . . not just us. That used to be nine-tenths of going out or having people in — the fun we had together, the sharing. Even when we were bored or an evening went badly, we'd look at each other, and each of us knew what the other was thinking, feeling, and experiencing. . . . Meg, sometimes living right in the same house with you, I feel walled away."

She said faintly, "But you're not." She wanted to say. "I don't feel that way," but she couldn't; it wasn't true. He could see her face only as a blur, but knew it to be anxious and protesting. "It's you," she said finally.

"Maybe it is. I'm sorry."

She put her hand out, touched his briefly as it lay on the wheel and said with an effort, "Maybe it isn't just you. . . . I don't know."

She did not. It was as if the origin of their difficulty and her unhappiness were no longer a vital factor. She no longer thought bitterly of the cause. Even her imagination rested; the painful, sickening, mental pictures had faded. What she thought of now was their present situation.

She said, in a stifled voice, "I don't think

264

of what happened any more, Davy . . . unless I'm reminded . . . I hardly ever — it's almost as if I'd read it somewhere. All I can think about now is what it did to you and to me and to our life together."

He said, "Yes, I know." And he did.

She was silent. She could not say: We can return to the bend in the road and start out again. She could not say: We have changed once, so there is no reason why we can't change again. She could only sit there quietly beside him, not believing in anything, not even in her prayers; she rarely prayed now — not believing in Davy or in herself or in their marriage — faith, too, seemed lost. When they reached the house, she went in and upstairs and he put the car away. When he came back, she heard him whistle for Corky; after a while he returned from their little walk and she heard him lock up, switch off the lights, and come up the stairs.

In their room he said, "Meg, suppose we go away for a while . . . maybe it's a little late for Canada, or early for Florida. What about North Carolina?"

She was already in bed. Now she sat up and repeated blankly, "Go away?"

"Yes . . . Things are going all right at the plant. I'm sure I could have a leave of absence for two or three weeks." He looked at her gravely. "Perhaps we can work things out if we can get away from here and be alone. I've already spoken to George Bemis and he seemed to think it could be arranged. I set no date, of course."

Meg shook her head. She said after a moment, "I don't think it would solve anything, Davy — if, as you believe, there's something to solve. I told you tonight, it's past, it's forgotten."

She thought: To go away with Davy alone as they'd done, a few times in their lives — among strange people, strange places, just themselves talking, laughing, looking across a table, lying in each other's arms . . . ?

But she couldn't because she was afraid. She thought: You can't go back; it wouldn't be the same; nothing ever is.

CHAPTER 16

One of the dreariest spots on life's road is the point of conviction that nothing will ever again happen to you. Oh, people will be born, marry, and die, within your circle of acquaintance; there will be illness, trivial or serious, yours or that of someone else; there may be depressions and recessions, when a man can lose his job overnight, given proper notice and severance pay. There could very well be war. Any one or all of these events must touch and in some way alter you. But what Davy was thinking, during the next few days was that nothing secret, personal, or profound was likely to reach him. He had always had a sense of excitement at the core of things, a turn-a-corner feeling, and sudden flashes of an almost intolerable happiness, which seemed causeless and for which there was no outward reason; and just as often the equally deep sense of sorrow, for which, again, there'd be no explicable source.

He remembered talking about this to his grandfather and asking for an explanation since, in childhood, these experiences had occurred more frequently than in maturity. He also remembered the smile which briefly curved his grandfather's straight mouth and irradiated the black eyes as he answered, "I can't explain it to you, Davy, except perhaps it's the spirit in you speaking."

Which had made matters more unfathomable than ever.

He considered, too, Meg's statement that she rarely thought of the origin of their difficulty. Whether she had been lying to herself, to him, or them both, he did not know. And now it did not much matter. A city can be destroyed by the flickering of a small candle.

Sometimes he reconstructed his last personal conversation with Rhoda Howard; he'd since seen her only with other people. She was, of course, right, he concluded; he was no more in love with her than she with him; attraction, he had admitted, and so had she; affection he assumed; yes, affection. He was in love only with what she appeared to stand for and embody: quietude, kindness, a reasonable attitude toward life, and acceptance of it.

But what if he met a woman with whom he could fall irrevocably in love?

He would not, he told himself; but even if he did, what then?

It had taken fourteen years to build what he'd believed to be a solid marriage, happy and rewarding, and a few minutes to tear down the structure. After a fashion, the walls still stood, but the foundation was shaken; the windows through which they had once looked for light, were gone; and the roof which once they had thought so secure, was unstable.

A few days later, as he came out of the conference room, Mrs. Easton met him, looking anxious. She said, "Mrs. Jones called; it's important that you get in touch with her immediately."

Later it seemed to him unpardonable that he did not leap to the conclusions which would have seemed natural: Meg was ill; she was going to the hospital; the house was burning; someone they loved had died. . . . But no, he'd thought first of Corky. He thought: *Corky's been hit.*

When he reached Meg, she said, "I told Mrs. Easton not to bring you out of conference."

"She didn't. It was over; I was leaving. What's happened?"

"Amy called. Edwin's had a bad attack; he's in the hospital in oxygen, and she wants me there."

"Of course she does, and you should be.

I'll come right home."

"It isn't necessary, Davy. I've packed — if I need more, Mrs. Lowry can send it later. I'll just drive on out."

He hung up. He was grieved because she no longer desired the accustomed shoulder to cry upon. If this had happened a couple of years ago, she would have been distracted. He could have seen to everything for her. She would probably have asked him to go with her.

He drove home, expecting she would have left, but risking the chance that she hadn't; nor had she. The station wagon was in the driveway. Mrs. Lowry was in the house, calm in any emergency, taking oral directions, writing things down, and as he walked in Meg was saying, ". . . that's the list. I'd be grateful if you could manage to do the shopping; you could phone and they could deliver whatever is necessary when you're here."

"Yes. Let me see now. Groceries, laundry, cleaner . . . we're almost out of dog food, Mrs. Jones."

Meg looked up as Davy came in, and said, "Isn't it lucky Mrs. Lowry can give us extra time? I'm sorry, though, you'll have to shift for yourself, mostly."

"I can still cook and make a bed. How bad is this?"

"A coronary and serious I'm afraid. Amy is quite beside herself, and that's so unlike her. She wants me to take over the house — not that I'll be popular in that department, I suppose — and, of course, there are things to do for the children."

"They're back in school?"

"Yes . . . but Hilary ships her laundry home and there are the phone calls and letters . . ."

"Amy isn't sending for the children?"

"No, she doesn't want them here, at least not now. . . . Oh dear," said Meg. "I never could keep a checkbook straight."

"Why should you?"

"Amy says I'm to pay bills. Of course she'll sign the checks. She's staying at the hospital; I'll see her every day. I can go down and talk to her in the reception room."

Presently, he followed her from the kitchen and upstairs to where her bags were packed and locked. He said, "I'll put these in the car. Please tell Amy how sorry I am . . . and that, if she needs me, she must let me know. Call me, Meg, every night, will you?"

"You may be out."

"Not every night and never late. And there's the office. Meg, are you certain you don't want me to go with you?"

"No, thanks just the same, but it wouldn't do any good . . ."

"I'd just be in the way," he said, reading her thought, "but I could run errands and drive cars and provide perhaps a little" — he hesitated over the word — "companionship."

"I know."

"If you need me, dear . . ."

"I'm sure I won't," Meg said, "unless something happens," and he thought: The euphemisms again. "Then, I'll call you at once."

They stood looking at each other across the two pieces of luggage. Corky was there regarding the suitcase and cosmetic case with great apprehension. Meg stooped to pat him; she said soothingly, "Davy's staying here, Corky."

Now there was nothing left to say except the things a woman always says to her husband when she leaves her house for an indefinite period: Remember to lock up, and to close the windows when you go out. . . . Mrs. Lowry will manage as best she can. . . . I expect the furnace people will come out to check the burner; they'll telephone first. . . . Your suits should be back from the cleaner's soon. . . . Remind Mrs. Lowry about the electric blankets, we could need them soon."

Now was the time to take her in his arms, hold her close and kiss her, but he could not seem to manage the few short steps that would bridge the distance between them. He picked up the bags and went downstairs ahead of her and put them into the trunk of the car.

Meg got in behind the wheel, leaned out the rolled-down window, and offered him her cheek. "Good-by," she said.

"Promise you'll call?"

She nodded, and the car drove off in a scatter of gravel.

Davy went back to the house for a moment and Mrs. Lowry called him. "In case you'd rather not eat out tonight, Mr. Jones, I'll leave you a casserole. Mrs. Jones suggested it, and said to remind you there are steaks and chops in the deep freeze."

He started back to the office, illogically angry that Meg could take the time to worry about his digestive tract. . . . Man does not live by bread alone, even the very best bread.

When he returned from the office, Corky bounced out of the yard to greet him, and they went into the house together. It was impersonally empty, as it had been the last time Meg went to Amy's. . . . No, it wasn't empty; it was filled with a nebulous freedom.

He took his time showering and changing into a sport shirt, slacks, and a sweater. This was the warmest September he could re-member, and they were practically at the end of it. He came downstairs, fixed Corky's supper and put it out of his reach.

"Are you nuts?" Corky inquired, madly and futilely leaping.

"No," said Davy. "I'm fixing myself a drink and taking it to the terrace. Wouldn't you rather dine there, alfresco?"

He made the drink, found some crackers, a hunk of good sharp cheese and a knife, and went out to set himself a small table. Returning, he retrieved Corky's dinner and they settled down where the sun was warm enough but not too warm.

"I could have worn shorts," he said to Corky.

Corky didn't care; he always wore shorts, with feather trim.

Why hadn't Meg telephoned when she reached New Jersey? He should have asked her to do that. No, she should damned well think of it herself.

He'd brought home the evening papers and a report he wanted to read and he settled back in the long chair. Corky looked up from his meal — How can they eat so fast? Davy asked himself — and barked reproachfully. Davy got up and went inside to bring out the bowl of water he'd forgotten.

Few people, if any, talk and think like characters in novels. A man and woman, involved in what to them, at least, appears a serious situation, discuss it, and even think about it, in a series of clichés. Davy stayed on the terrace looking at the disturbing headlines, at photographs of alleged actresses, whose talents were confirmed by tape measure, next to pictures of bomb shelters. He looked at obituaries and baseball scores, at the cartoons and the stock-market figures. His stocks had done well, over the last year, as had those he'd given Meg; she has a little pile of her own, he reflected, in addition to a small trust fund.

He fished for a pencil, found none and started to do figures in his mind: his present salary; his future salary with the present firm or — if he ever decided to change his job — elsewhere; the dividends from stocks, provided they continued; life insurance and what was in the savings bank.

Instead of totaling up to a sum it came out another cliché: We can't go on like this.

That is to say, he could not. If he were stark alone, he would not be as lonely, in the way which most mattered.

He told himself, again, as the ice melted in the glass, that it was not Meg's retreat from physical love which had brought him, by an almost imperceptible progression, to the conclusion that he could no longer live with her.

At first he had been greatly troubled and unhappy but he had, to the best of his capacity, understood. He could approximately put himself in her place by thinking: Suppose it had been Meg and a strange man in that motel? How would I have felt? It was only an approximation because he could not remotely imagine it, except as a hypothetical circumstance; and, you had to face it, biologically there is a difference; a woman seduced, if you wish to phrase it in that way; a man, surrendering. Some might phrase it in reverse. But it was hardly an accurate yardstick.

Then, when she suddenly turned aggressor in their most personal relationship, he had been unable to comprehend and had felt, after a while, only discomfort and uneasy embarrassment; he'd been admittedly relieved when that phase of her emotional expression had ceased, but after a time her resigned, passive and — yes — dutiful behavior had begun to revolt him.

But he was growing used to it. He supposed that he could live with it for the rest of their lives. If you are hungry enough, you grow to recognize the hunger as a simple need, and forget to mourn over the lost quality of what once had fed you.

The important thing to him was that they appeared to have lost each other, or, rather, lost that which was essential in each, and which had been mutely shared, beyond the intimacy of their bodies. It requires time for most men and women to grow into a companionship of minds; and even longer to achieve the true rapport, a communion of individual spirits. It is rare, this final marriage, and many never achieved it. He had thought that despite surface differences, he and Meg had between them found something of value. Believing it now to be gone, he asked himself if it had ever existed or if he had only taken it for granted that it had? If it were gone, he did not think it possible to live in, and with, such sterility.

He went back into the house with Corky beside him, and looked into the oven where he had put Mrs. Lowry's casserole at the proper temperature, she having left him directions written in her round, careful hand. He made coffee and a salad and presently took his tray to the kitchen table, where he ate leisurely and read the report.

When the telephone rang, he answered it in the kitchen and Meg said, "Davy . . . they think Edwin's holding his own. Amy's at the hospital, of course, and she'll stay there until he's out of danger."

"Are you all right?" he asked her, after he had made the usual comments.

"Oh, yes, although it's queer being here without Amy and, of course, I worry . . . but the staff's most helpful. I don't have much to do really, except, be here. Amy calls me every so often and tomorrow I'll probably go down and talk to her outside of Edwin's room. Naturally, I'm awfully concerned."

"So am I."

There was a pause. Neither one said, "Darling"; neither one said, "I miss you." Davy didn't say, "Please, let me come and be with you"; and Meg didn't say, "Will you think me foolish if I ask you to come?"

But after a moment Davy did say, "Keep in touch." Meg promised to and they said good-by. Davy added, "Take care of yourself."

When they had hung up, he finished his supper, washed up, and went into the living room with the report in his hand. Corky stationed himself in front of the television set, looking expectantly over his shoulder. He was very fond of television, particularly Westerns. But Davy did not move. It was dark and he'd switched on only one light. After a while, because of Corky's entreaties, he turned on the set, went out and made himself a stiff drink, and returned to watch, without seeing them, the innocuous pictures on the screen. When the telephone rang, he was in no hurry to answer it.

"Oh," said Rhoda. "Davy? I told Meg I'd call her."

"She's away," he said shortly. Rhoda was part of another world, he thought.

"Will she be back by Sunday? I'm going to have a buffet lunch after church, and I hoped you'd both come."

"I don't know when she'll be home," answered Davy. "Amy — you remember her sister Amy; she was here not long ago . . . ?"

"I didn't meet her," Rhoda said, "I saw her, though — is she ill?"

"No, her husband is. He's had a coronary, so Meg's gone to New Jersey to help out."

"I'm so sorry," Rhoda said in her warm voice. "Will you tell her so when you talk with her . . . and ask her to call me when she returns?"

She didn't say: If she's still away Sunday, you come to the lunch; she didn't suggest: Now you're alone, come to dinner some evening.

Intelligent woman, Mrs. Howard; a thoroughly nice woman and very desirable, he thought in a detached way.

Later, he walked with Corky out on the terrace and looked up at the quiet stars, burning with their own secret silver life — if, in this era even a star dared have one — and realized, with a sense of shock, how indifferent he was. "Take care of yourself," he'd told Meg, an admonition he'd used to her a thousand times. Now — just a phrase. He'd traveled from self-abasement and guilt to grief and a sort of horror, and from there to fluctuating moods of anger, anxiety, and sorrow. What remained was indifference. It went deeper than boredom and everything over and above it, he felt, was like drifting shadows — on the surface of the stream, not affecting the depth.

Well, he thought, if that's so, then you can stay here with Meg until you die, and not care.

That was the ultimate step; the not caring, the not caring at all. He thought, walking to the edge of the terrace and noticing the dew was heavy beyond it: I must cut the grass . . . and told himself that he couldn't stay anywhere with anyone, not caring and wholly objective.

He spoke aloud and Corky came running back to him; he said bewildered, and not by alcohol, "But I don't understand it, when I love her."

Now he could also regard love with detachment; there it was; immutable at the core, yet it offered him nothing, no sense of fulfillment, or of integration, and at this moment not even the sense of loss.

So you went to work and came home, you loved your wife and yet you were barricaded from her, from your work, and your friends — even from growing old, and from living itself — because you had become unconcerned. It was, he told himself, wholly illogical.

He went up to bed to read, although reading was no longer the pleasurable adventure he'd always found it. He could feel need, for food and drink, for exercise, for laughter and recreation and for the outward expression of love. He could, he knew, at times feel irritation, anger, grief, and anxiety. Yet all were shadows on the stream. Beneath the shadows, those of the ripples caused by something or someone outside himself, the dark current of his spiritual being now ran, insensible and undisturbed.

CHAPTER 17

His book did not hold his attention, but it was something to look at. Television was something to look at, too, but all the time your inward eyes would be turned toward yourself.

The light from the single lamp made curious shadows in the room. Corky wandered in, the door having been left open, and remarked that it was getting pretty late. Davy agreed, but sent him back to bed and he went without murmur toward the basket in the hall and the comfort of the much-chewed toy which was his doggy substitute for the blanket. His tail drooped, his ears sagged, but he knew better than to cry up a storm. However, he was muttering to himself. "If," he was saying, "you're going to stay up all night, you need company, don't you? How about going down to the kitchen for a snack?"

He sat at the head of the stairs and emitted one inquiring bark. "No," said Davy, from the bedroom, and Corky drooped and sagged his way to the basket and the toy. Occasionally, in a time which seemed now prehistoric, Davy and Meg had taken themselves downstairs at unlikely hours, with Corky padding ahead of them, and all three had looked hopefully in the refrigerator. There'd been times, too, when Davy and Corky went alone, given official permission by Meg's, "You boys run along and stuff yourselves. I'm too sleepy."

Davy got up, shut the door and then went back to bed. A sleeping pill? No, he decided. All it would do for him was to push him over the cliff into a heavy darkness, from which he would awaken, tired and foggy. And, heaven knew, he was foggy enough without that added extra.

A decent man, he thought, doesn't walk away from his responsibilities, his wife, his job and his community, simply because, on an April night, he had repudiated for a brief space of time all that these represented to him.

But, he argued — his hands behind his head, the book on the floor — I'm walking out, every day, if not physically. You can walk away to remote distances, mentally, emotionally, and spiritually . . . it's only the physical you, the least important, which remains.

Suddenly, he was sleepy; he turned out the light and slept, but in an hour woke.

After a while, he rose and turned on the small television set, recessed into a bookcase, which he'd given Meg one Christmas. They used it very little and, now, lying there with one subdued light above the screen, he watched, without interest, a cops-and-robbers movie. It did not make him sleepy again; it merely irritated him. He turned off the set and went into the bathroom. There were plenty of sleeping pills there, those Mike had given him, and Meg's, which Mike had prescribed when last she'd seen him for a checkup and complained of increasing insomnia. They'd come in very handy, for her, Davy reflected.

He took a bottle in his hand and looked at the colored capsules, remembering that when, more than once, he'd spoken to her in the night: "Meg? You awake? Let's talk . . ." she had been sleeping soundly. In addition to alleviating her insomnia they had provided a marvelous excuse for her, an escape.

He took the prescribed two and then went back to bed. As he turned off the light, he heard the whisper at the door. He went to it and said, "I'm all right, Corky. Go back to sleep, there's a good guy."

Although he'd had the pills for some time, he had rarely taken them and had not built up a tolerance; therefore they soon began to affect him with the pleasant, floating drowsiness, the inability to think clearly, and eventually the unterrifying plunge over the cliff.

Sometime, just before dawn, the telephone bell wakened him and he erupted from a seemingly endless dream, groggy, a little dazed, and groped for the instrument, which was lighted at the base. But when he said, "Hello — hello," there was no answer, just the dial sound, and he fell back into the pillows and the dream again.

He overslept, but fortunately it was not one of Mrs. Lowry's days. When he got up, he made himself a pot of black coffee and attended to Corky's needs. Sitting at the kitchen table, he was conscious that, in a fragmentary blurred fashion, he recalled something of his dream.

Meg and himself, at the Lake, rowing for a shore which kept receding; Meg and himself on the wonderful short trip they'd taken years ago, to the Caribbean. In that part of the dream there was a swimming pool. In another part, he remembered walking with Meg in a city he'd never seen before and she was asking, "Is it Athens?" In yet another, he was with her in their first apartment. Then, walking down an aisle — was it a church or was it a mosque? — he'd looked down and found he had no shoes.

Other people drifted in and out of the dream, some of whom he'd forgotten, but Amy was there, saying, "When Edwin dies, I'll be a handsome widow," and Bob was there saying something at which everyone laughed uproariously. Rhoda came and looked around a table crowded with people, smiled, and went away. And Mike took Davy's blood pressure and said, "You'll live a hundred years, you poor bastard."

In the dream there was a small woman with a mask over her eyes. She came and went; but Meg was always there. Yet when he moved to touch or speak to her, she wasn't. He asked, "May I have this dance?" and she answered, "Of course, darling," but when he took her in his arms, it was someone he'd never seen before.

The drug, of course, he told himself, drinking his coffee, and probably just before I woke, after the telephone call — I wonder if that was Meg . . . ? That kind of drug-induced dream can't have significance, psychiatry notwithstanding. Or has it?

Who had telephoned at that unearthly hour? Someone, he reasoned, who expected a familiar voice, and, hearing a strange one, had hung up, rather than apologize. It seemed to him that he could recall a second's silence and then the definitive click before the dial sound went on again. Somehow . . . he had expected to hear Meg's voice . . .

It troubled him and during the morning he asked Mrs. Easton to get Mrs. Jones for him.

"Meg?"

"Yes. Is anything wrong?" she asked.

"No. Everything's fine. How's Edwin?"

He'd talked to her on the previous evening, of course, and now she said, "There's been no change. He was holding his own yesterday, as I told you. They're going to let me just stand in the door and wave today. Amy phoned a few minutes ago; she says she'll start coming home nights now. She says she feels as if she'd been under a steam roller."

"I bet she does." He hesitated. How absurd can you get? . . . He'd ask it anyway. So he did. "Meg, you didn't call me this morning, did you? I didn't look at the clock, but it must have been before five!"

"Why . . . no."

"Someone did. I was asleep and by the time I got around to answering, whoever it was hung up. It scared me. I thought Edwin —"

"I wouldn't call you at that hour, Davy,

unless there was an emergency."

"I know; that's what worried me —"

"In which case," she concluded logically, "I certainly wouldn't have hung up."

They spoke for a few minutes longer and then said good-by.

He was stupid to think that Meg had called him, and then hung up; yet somehow this morning he'd thought so. Looking into his coffee cup as if it were a crystal ball, he'd almost convinced himself . . .

Well, so, O.K., wrong number. She must think him out of his mind. There was no reason for her to call him — except in reference to Edwin — at any hour.

The days went by; they always do; and they do not return, not ever, which is something most human beings endeavor to forget. Davy went to dinner at the Club with men from the office, also temporary bachelors, and with George Bemis and his wife. There were a couple of poker games, once at his house. He played some golf and was, he perceived, not only off his game, but drinking a little too much; not enough to affect him seriously at the time, or next morning, yet more than usual.

He could recognize this and evaluate it and establish the reasons; not merely the transient escape, and certainly no form of one-hundred-proof, rose-colored glasses, slipped on and off, but mainly a loosening, for the moment of tension, and an attempt to free himself from constant subterranean preoccupation with his personal situation.

He continued to call Meg daily and latterly had asked her, now that Edwin was gaining every day, when he could expect her to come home? She answered: "As soon as I can." Pressed, she explained that Amy still needed her.

It was during the last of such conversations that he told her with some desperation, "I need you, too, Meg."

She was silent, and then spoke of other things.

But he wondered, when he had replaced the instrument: Do I, really? He had, God knew, for months, but not now; no, not now. That night, in the cool of an October evening following a mellow day, as he and Corky walked on the terrace and about the grounds, he told himself that what he needed was to get away, clear away. He said so aloud and in reply Corky barked that he'd be better off watching "Gunsmoke."

Davy thought: There are other jobs, particularly one in Boston he'd been offered recently and which was still unfilled — he'd taken pains to ferret that much out. There were also other states, a lot of them, and many other countries.

That night he went to bed resolved to take what he told himself would amount to a marital coffee break. He could not — as once he'd considered doing — walk out for good. Not now, at any rate. He'd go away, by himself, for a while. Later, if he and Meg could come to some agreement, he might return. The thought crossed his mind that perhaps she would prefer that he didn't come back. In that case, they would have to see what could be made of their lives — separately.

He could arrange for a leave of absence, he'd already spoken of it to Bemis, and his assistant was perfectly capable; too capable, perhaps. But Davy had never taken long vacations; he was entitled to some extra time off. He could go to his club in New York; he rarely entered it unless he had to be in the city on business, and then only for lunch or dinner. But he could stay there; he'd paid his dues since his graduation from the university.

When Meg came back, he must tell her that it was impossible to continue in this fashion. Perhaps a compromise could be reached; or, if she agreed with him, the solution would not be difficult. He would leave it to her: Separation, legal or otherwise; or, divorce? The house was in her name. She could sell it and move away, or continue to live in it. If the position in Boston did not work out, there would be others; he had been approached more than once in the past few years.

He had lunch with Bemis that day and Bemis asked, "When are you planning to take your extra holiday? Have you and Meg decided where to go?"

"No," said Davy, and told him about Meg's continued absence and the reason. He added, "But it will be straightened out within a day or so. . . . Would it be possible for me to go the first of next week?"

It was possible, said Bemis, thinking that something was wrong; he'd liked to know what was the matter, he said. Davy hadn't been himself for weeks.

Davy's heart accelerated. He said, "Nothing. I'm tired, I suppose, and working on an ulcer, that's all."

On Sunday night he called Meg. She said that she thought she'd be home soon, but to expect her when he saw her.

Monday began Davy's extra two weeks. . . . He spent the day with Corky outdoors, taking a long walk, and indoors, putting his personal house in order.

That night, after dinner, he wrote a letter to Meg. He rewrote it a number of times, the wastebasket was full of torn sheets of paper, covered with his small, clear writing. These he burned in the fireplace while Corky sat looking at him anxiously.

Finally he wrote:

Meg:

I am going away for a time. I'm taking the holiday I spoke to you about; it began today. You can reach me in town at my club. There's sure to be considerable speculation about my absence. George takes it for granted that we are going away on a trip together; it was what I originally had in mind. But you did not want to go.

This is not a sudden decision; it has been shaping up for a long while. When I say, flatly, that I cannot live with you; I mean, not in the same house, under present conditions.

I have made you very unhappy. I have seen you suffer, and it has hurt me as nothing else I've ever known. What I did, I did — as I have told you over and over — without extenuation. It was a casual contact, nothing more, and less important than brushing one's teeth. With the woman — whom I'd never seen before and, God willing, never shall again — it may have been more; an urgency, a need. Yet it was not important to her either; it was trivial.

My biggest mistake lay in telling you of something which meant nothing to me, but I knew that you would feel differently, and I couldn't, I thought, exist as a whole person under the load of guilt and self-reproach that such knowledge imposed on me. Now I can no longer exist, as a whole person, under the burden of your daily, implicit — if often unspoken — forgiveness, for there has been no forgetting.

While I'm away, I'll try to get my thoughts straightened out, after a fashion, and to emerge somehow from this confusion. My leave of absence is for two weeks; at the end of it, or before, I'll come back to the house and we will talk, reasonably I hope, of the next steps we must take together or separately.

I realize how you felt, or still feel, about Rhoda. There has been no reason. She is a fine woman and one who, out of her sorrow and loss, has achieved understanding, which is, I believe, the most important quality anyone can possess. I have not confided in her, although I'm sure you believe that I have. Once I was tempted to, but she stopped me. She did not wish to hear anything of a personal nature. She surmised, of course, it had to do with you. But she is your friend and loyal to you. You told me once that I was in love with her. I am not. I have never been in love with anyone except you. I love her in the way a person loves a horizon, a great tree, a garden — quietly and with appreciation. But in no other way. She is my friend, too, and within the framework of that relationship, I believe she is fond of me.

I have loved only you — and wholly.

Therefore, whatever you decide, whatever you want to do, you must, but I cannot return to this life of shadows, which in the last analysis is no life at all.

If you do not wish me to return to the house, if you do not care to see or talk with me, all right; that too can be arranged, in which case I could advise you to see Seth Adams. We both like him, and he is, as you know, clever, compassionate, and discreet.

It is inadequate to say that I am sorry, and that I'll never forgive myself. I never should have told you of an incident so unimportant to me, but I never kept secrets from you and, although I knew it would cause your unhappiness, I did not realize that it would seem large enough to you to erase fourteen years. . . .

Davy

He got up and stretched; he felt as if he had been on a long journey. He had not been able to say in the letter all he thought, felt, and experienced. Communication between individuals, peoples, nations, he thought, is so difficult. You write something — or say it; you know what you mean; the words you use are in the dictionary; but the person reading or listening finds his own meaning, even though he, too, has access to the same dictionary.

He looked at the clock. It was not yet nine. He put the letter in an envelope, sealed it, put it in his pocket, went to the telephone, and dialed Rhoda's number.

A servant answered and he gave his name; and presently she spoke to him. He said abruptly. "This is Davy. Do you have company tonight?"

"Company," the lovely, old-fashioned word; nowadays one said "guests."

"Why, no. I'm alone, reading. Is anything

wrong? Has Meg's brother-in-law — ?"

He broke in, saying, "He's better. I'm going away, Rhoda. I'd like very much to see you — now, if possible. It's urgent."

She said quietly, "All right. I'll expect you."

He took Corky with him, drove to Rhoda's and left Corky in the car. He didn't want to think about Corky. He remembered Bob's joking about "custody of the canine. . . ."

There was a fire on the hearth, in Rhoda's big living room and the heat drew out the lovely fragrance of roses.

Rhoda said, "You look wretched. Can I fix you a drink?"

"I'd like that," he said.

"Scotch?"

"Yes — a light one."

When she brought it to him, he put it on the table beside him. Later, he remembered that he drank very little of it. And Rhoda asked, sitting opposite, "What's happened, Davy?"

"I'm going away for a little while," he said painfully. "When Meg returns — and I don't know how much longer she'll be away — I wish you'd help her, Rhoda. You can; and she'll need help."

Rhoda said, "If she comes to me, I'll try." She looked at him gravely. She asked,

"You're going away . . . you mean you're leaving — for good?"

He steadied his hand and lit a cigarette. "Such an unrevealing expression," he said. " 'For good' — yes. Whether for good in the sense of forever, or not, I suppose it could amount to that. Oh, I'll come back presently," he said heavily, "and make an attempt to talk things over with Meg — if she'll agree to see me. There are a lot of things to be settled."

Rhoda said, looking into the secret life of the fire, "I don't quite understand, Davy."

"Once I started to tell you."

"I remember, I didn't want you to, and I don't now."

He said, "There has to be a reason for everything, even if people — and the world itself — aren't very reasonable. I won't give you a blow-by-blow version, if that's what you're afraid of. Sometime ago I did something which Meg, after I'd told her, found unpardonable. Yet" — he put the cigarette in the ash tray — "she forgives me daily. I told you this once. She says she's forgotten, but she hasn't."

"I remember," Rhoda said after a moment, "and I told you that the only true forgiveness is to remember and still forgive. Now, I'm going to tell you something, Davy.

Hal isn't my son — physically; but he is Sam's."

He could only look at her, too astonished to speak.

She said, "Everyone at home knows we adopted Hal — the Warings know it, here. There's no secret about the adoption. But with the exception of a very few people, including Hal himself, no one knows he's Sam's son."

"I don't understand," he said.

"It's simple enough," she told him, smiling. "We'd been married five years when Sam met a girl. How he met her, and who she was, is of no importance. It was a short affair and he told me about it after it was over. I gave him a very bad time. The girl, meanwhile, had left Denver and gone elsewhere. She had great courage. Sam did not know she was pregnant. It wasn't until Hal was four — she'd been supporting him, God knows how — that she learned she was incurably ill, and wrote to Sam."

"Then," Davy said, still incredulous, "You never had a child?"

"No. I couldn't have children; that fact was established by exceedingly good doctors. One of the few difficulties Sam and I had was just that. He wanted children, particularly a son. But he accepted it. I didn't.

When you told me Meg would not adopt a child, I was so sorry. In our case, it was Sam who didn't want to adopt children."

"But how could he, how could he do that to you?" he thought aloud. "Just five years —"

"I married young," she said. "I finished law school afterward. Oh, not very young, of course, but I was immature in many ways, and it was difficult for me to adjust to a number of things. In this girl Sam found excitement. . . . The affair was of very short duration, Davy . . . anyway when her letter came, he went to the place where she was living and brought Hal back to me."

"Did he tell you he was going to?"

"No," said Rhoda, "he didn't."

"But I don't see how you could have accepted —"

"I didn't either. But he was Sam's son. Then, after a while, he was mine." Her face was luminous with love. "No woman," she said, "has ever had a better."

"And he knows about this?"

"Oh, yes. At first, he knew only that he was adopted. He was old enough, of course, to remember his mother, for a while anyway. Then, when Hal was older — not long before Sam died, he told him. That's how I know about forgiving, Davy. First you don't forgive at all; then you make a sacrificial gesture of trying to forgive; you tell yourself, you forget; finally you forgive and remember what you've forgiven — and nevertheless forgive. Sam loved me," she said, still with that radiance about her, "and I loved him. I still do. . . ."

Davy got to his feet. He said, "It's hard to know what to say."

"Don't try. Go away if you must, but come back. Meantime if Meg comes to me, I'll do what I can."

She went with him to the door and he said, "Thank you for telling me. More than anyone I know, I admire and respect you, Rhoda."

"Sam did, too," she said.

CHAPTER 18

On the way home Davy stopped at Mrs. Lowry's. She lived some distance from his house, in an elderly dwelling set back from the street. He knew — he'd heard her say often enough — that she never went to bed until midnight or after, what with ironing and television. She was a dedicated television buff.

He got out of the car, told Corky to come along. The shades were not drawn and as they went up the wooden steps of the porch he saw Mr. Lowry — it seemed incredible that there was a Mr. Lowry — moving about the living room, a beer can in his hand. Mrs. Lowry was sitting in front of the set, which, even from outside, Davy and Corky could hear.

The door was opened to Davy's knock and Corky smiled with pleasure when he saw his good friend standing there.

"Why, Mr. Jones," said Mrs. Lowry, astonished. "Hi, Corky," she added and stooped to pat him. She straightened up, looking troubled. "Is anything the matter —"

"No," Davy told her. "I just want to talk to you."

"Won't you come in?"

"No, thanks, Mrs. Lowry, I just want to ask a favor. I've been called out of town. I'll have to go tonight, and Mrs. Jones isn't home yet. I don't know just when she'll return, but I'm sure it will be soon. May I leave Corky with you until she comes back? He's had his supper. He'll be all right until tomorrow. I know you'll be at the house then, and there's plenty for him there; then if you'll take him home again with you when you leave. . . . I'm sorry I wasn't able to plan this in advance."

Mrs. Lowry said she'd be glad to have Corky, for as long as necessary. He'd be company for Mr. Lowry who was round the house, mostly — except for odd jobs — now he'd retired.

Her tall shambling husband came to the door. Davy knew him by sight. They spoke to each other and Mr. Lowry snapped his fingers at Corky who ran inside to watch TV with him. Mrs. Lowry said, "He won't be strange, like at the vet's. He knows me." She added, "when I saw you standing out here I was afraid Mr. Mason —"

"He's doing fine," Davy assured her. Don't make a production of this, he admonished himself. Don't go in and say anything to Corky. You're just going out of town for a bit. Don't shake hands with Mrs. L and thank her for the past years and say, "Look after my wife."

Corky came back to the door and Davy said, "It's all right, fella; you stay here with Mrs. Lowry . . . see you later."

When he reached home, he went upstairs and packed a bag . . . enough to get along with and thought: When Meg gets back, she'll call me . . . and if she says . . . If she said what? Don't come? Come at once? Or: When will you come?

Suppose she didn't call?

He telephoned his club in the city and the man at the desk said they could accommodate him. How long would he be staying?

He said he didn't know.

It would make no sense to take his car. He'd have no use for it in New York and the club had no garage. What would he have use for in New York? Board and lodging, a place to go to at night. He doubted that he would know anyone staying there and it was unlikely he'd run into anyone he knew at lunch or dinner.

In a few days he would take a train, or fly, to Boston to talk to the people there. But he would have to wait until Meg called. No, he need not, he could leave word where he was and that he'd be gone, just overnight, perhaps, or simply, for the day.

He looked around the bedroom, and then went downstairs. It was strange that the books he hadn't been able to read were on the night table and that no flowers were about. He would walk out of his house, after checking to see if windows were closed, after locking up, and someday he would come back to it, to a different house, as a different man.

He remembered that he hadn't emptied the ash trays . . . but Mrs. Lowry would be there in the morning.

He walked to the station, and it was a long walk; also the night was cold. Today had been the first for some time when there had been very little sun, the first autumnal day, really. The wind was easterly and it was damp and cold; there was a bite in the air, sharp and unpleasant. He walked, not thinking of the distance. Walking was a mechanical process, and he hardly knew he was carrying the small bag.

The sky was cloudy, dark clouds scudding before the wind, and no stars shone. The clouds were fringed and looked ominous. He thought: I hope it's past hurricane weather time. The last storms had missed this locality, or almost.

Meg was afraid of storms, they made her nervous; they had been through several, some bad, since moving here. Corky hated them. He hid under beds.

When Davy reached the station, there was no one in it. It was a small frame structure with wooden benches and it smelled of dust and smoke and the lavatories. The news-stand was closed; so was the ticket office.

He had forgotten to look at a timetable, but he thought there would be one more train tonight. He took a folder from the shelf in front of the closed ticket window. Yes, there would be just one; it was due in an hour if it were on time. It was a local and stopped at every station. It was fortunate he'd told the club not to expect him until very late.

Davy sat down on a bench, his bag beside him and smoked, throwing the cigarettes on the floor, stamping them out, as, evidently, many had done before him. He had to have some sort of a plan. Perhaps an empty rail-way station is as good a place to think as any.

When Meg called — or wrote — on her return, he must ask if he could come to see her for a short time. He should have mentioned in the letter — he'd left it on her dressing table in the tradition of such letters

— that he'd told Mrs. Lowry he'd been called out of town and that he'd left Corky with her.

When he saw Meg — providing she'd see him — they would formulate their sober and reasonable plans. That is, she must make hers; his were already made.

He decided to wait a few days and then, if she had not called him, he could go to Boston.

Perhaps she would wonder tomorrow, the next day and for many days thereafter, why he didn't telephone her at Amy's. Perhaps she'd call Mrs. Lowry at the house, or, failing to reach her, call the office. Mrs. Easton would say that he'd gone away. How was that to be explained? He could see Mrs. Easton's eyebrows shooting up when she realized that Mrs. Jones knew nothing of his leave of absence or whatever one wanted to call it.

Well, there are always dangling ends and no scissors with which to cut them neatly.

A hundred details . . . they were like a shaken kaleidoscope in his mind, but not brightly colored bits, just the dark and somber ones. He thought of things to which at this point he had no answers. Would Meg stay in the house or not? That question made sense enough, but to wonder if she'd want him to keep up the Club membership was idiotic.

He thought of Rhoda. She was herself and Meg was herself; no one could teach Meg to forgive and remember. He thought then of that the day when Rhoda had said, "You might do some forgiving, you know," and he'd known that she meant forgive himself.

Forgive himself for what? For an April night in a motel, the name of which he'd forgotten?

But he had written Meg that he would never forgive himself — for telling her. . . .

The lights in this waiting room were unshielded. They glared down, without mercy, and his eyes hurt. He kept smelling the stale odors. How long ago had this station been built . . . fifty years, seventy-five? He found himself thinking of the people who left here and returned; the people who went to work and came back, the men whose wives brought them here, or who drove themselves and parked their cars in the inadequate space; the men who came back each evening, whose wives waited for them, with indifference, pleasure, expectancy. He thought of those who went only a short distance to another local station, youngsters going to school, kids off to their first jobs. He thought of other people for whom at this station some long journey began and felt in his mind and blood, the hurry, the anxiety, the boredom and the excitement, the joy and misery and above all the terrible patience of people and, always, the basic loneliness.

He felt a little sick and somewhat dizzy. A little more and he was afraid he would lose consciousness, here alone in the station. True, he had eaten little at dinner, but he had barely tasted the drink at Rhoda's — so it wasn't that. He shook his head to clear it, and reminded himself that everyone feels terribly alone at one time or another. Alone, you are born through a narrow channel of pain and, alone, you die . . . no matter how many are with you at the beginning and at the end . . . if it were the end. He simply didn't believe it was; it could not logically be. Such thinking had nothing to do with what he had been taught, with what he had always heard preached.

So, he reasoned further, no matter how much you loved or were loved, no matter how many relationships you knew in a lifetime, you were alone and, as a man alone, you were accountable to yourself and to whatever power you thought of as God. . . . And that brought him back again to the matter of forgiveness. God forgives, he thought.

Can a man, then, forgive himself? Can I, for instance, forgive myself . . . for telling her, of course? But beyond that, for what? God knows, I've suffered as much as she has.

After the wind, the earthquake, the fire, and the still small voice. It spoke to him now — and distinctly — through the blur of his emotional fatigue — he heard it.

A man, he thought, should be able to stand up to his own guilt, and to look upon the image of himself which his own act had destroyed. He had now to forgive himself for what he had done to Meg, putting the burden on her slender shoulders in order to straighten his own, poisoning the air she breathed so that he might breathe a fresher.

In this way he had thought to appease his conscience. How many times had he told her, and himself, that the April night was without meaning? If he really believed that, why had he allowed it to assume such proportions and, in the assumption, destroy not only his image in his own eyes and in Meg's, but destroy her as well?

Perhaps a hundred or a thousand or a million women would have thought it unimportant, too. He didn't know. Meg could never have thought so; she had always been disturbed by trivialities:

"Darling, what does it matter that you broke the pitcher?"

"But it was my grandmother's!"

He remembered innumerable such incidents in the past fourteen years: a careless cleaning woman, a tree that had died, a plant that wouldn't respond to care, a wrong hemline, the time her hair had been cut too short.

He told himself, "I've thought mainly of myself, and of the rebuilding of the image in my own eyes."

It all came back to the integral loneliness. He got up, leaving the bag on the bench, and went from the station to stand outside a moment looking at the dark sky and the darker-seeming, moving shapes of clouds. Then he went back again and sat down, thinking: The frustrations and failures, the sense sometimes of not belonging anywhere — everyone has these I suppose.

He was shaken with an extraordinary compassion for the world, the little world, and its people, each in his separate compartment, trying to reach out to others, to communicate and to belong.

A train from the city went by the little station without stopping. It spoke, in a deep mutter as it passed, going north, with its load of people — tired people, eager people — all going somewhere.

Now his compassion narrowed to Meg, who was, and always had been, insecure. An enormous tenderness shattered him. Her only security — deep, underneath all her trivialities — had been love . . . and now she believed she had lost it. . . . But she hadn't. He loved her. Perhaps somehow he could prove he did.

Suddenly he picked up his bag and walked swiftly from the close, quiet room. Marriage, he thought, is love. It is compromise, as Rhoda said, but more than anything, it is trust. When he reached the house, he would destroy the letter. He would never tell Meg about it. And, perhaps, if he were very fortunate, he would be able to rebuild, in some measure, that which he had destroyed.

He walked back along the lighted streets and the dark roads. He would telephone her. He didn't care how late it was. He didn't care if he frightened Amy out of her wits. He would telephone and say, "Let me speak to Meg," and when she answered he would say, "Have pity on me, come home."

He was nearly home when a car passed him and he recognized it — Meg's station wagon. It turned into his driveway and the garage light went on from outside.

Davy began to run, the bag bumping against his side. God, he thought, let me get

311

there, before she opens that letter

But when he had gone through the garage into the kitchen and run up the stairs, she was standing by the dressing table with the letter in her hand.

He asked, "Have you read it?"

"No." She looked at him; after a moment, she said, "You've been running."

"Meg" — he sat down on the edge of his bed, utterly spent — "I was at the station . . . I was going away . . . and then I knew it was impossible. So I came back, first to telephone you and ask you to come home, and then to destroy that letter."

She weighed it in her hand; otherwise she did not move, and he looked at her without hope. It seemed to him that she looked . . . not older . . . but more mature.

She said, "I did call you early the other morning, Davy. Then I was afraid and hung up."

"Meg."

She said in a slow, wondering voice, "But, I came back —"

"You didn't telephone, you didn't say —"

"I didn't know. I just — left. Amy thought I'd gone crazy. I threw things into the car and got in and drove. I had to get home. I thought: If I don't go home right away, I'll die." Suddenly she was down on the floor beside him, her arms about his knees, her face looking up. She said, "I've missed you so much and for so long. I was so lonely, Davy."

He stroked her bright, silky hair. The tears were running down his cheeks, but he did not know it. He said, "I love you, Meg; I always have, I always shall . . . read the letter."

It was on the floor. She picked it up and then rose, looking taller than she was, looking — what was the word? — proud? Yes, proud.

She put the envelope in his hands. She said, "Tear it up, Davy. I don't want to read it . . . it's not that I'm afraid . . . I just don't want to. We can talk about it later, if you want."

He got to his feet and put his arms around her. She leaned against him heavily. Then she said, before he kissed her, "If you'd like, if you still want to, perhaps we could go away?"

Much later he went to open a window and Meg came and stood beside him. She looked out, and said, "It's clearing."

The dark clouds were still there, but they had thinned and had drifted away from the silver faces of the stars and Meg said sleepily, "It's Mrs. Lowry's day."

Davy looked from the window and was aware that the wind had changed; cool, and freshening, it was blowing from the West.

"Come back to bed, darling," he said. "You must get some sleep."